AN ICICLE
Made for Two

An Icicle Made for Two

© copyright 2026 J.P. Sterling

Editors: Rebecca Carpender and Barren Acres Editing

CONTENTS

Blurb

Single momhood put my love life on the bench until billionaire Bill Baker skated in.

I've always put my son first—every carpool, every budget cut, every hockey practice at insane hours.

His dream?

Playing pro hockey.

Mine?

A nap.

So, when rumors swirl about a new AHL team landing in our tiny town of Mapleton, both our ears perk up. Noah gets a tryout. I get public humiliation after mistaking the team owner for the janitor.

That should've been the end of it. But apparently, fate is a fan of awkward encounters, because I keep running into the guy.

Again.

And again.

We start to connect through shared interests, and it turns out he's actually a nice guy.

The real problem?

It's too bad falling for the billionaire who holds my son's future in his hands is a penalty I can't afford.

An *Icicle Made for Two* is a billionaire, single mom, sweet hockey romcom with HEA that is filled with that "we shouldn't—but we totally might" tension.

One

Bill Baker

My heart slams against my chest as I drop to my knee, exactly the way I've practiced for months. My sweating palm trembles as I pinch my late grandmother's diamond ring in my fingers at the perfect angle.

In a textbook reaction, just like the movies, Lacy gasps, her hand flying over her mouth. Tears well up in her eyes as she peers down at me. If I pause for any reason, I'll lose my nerve, which is silly because there is no reason to be scared. I have loved Lacy all through high school.

We are meant to be together.

Ever since I've learned I'm moving to another city to realize my dream of playing in the NHL, I'm overcome with such a heavy emotional weight, I'm stuck. My chest cinches so tightly. The thought of leaving Lacy makes me not want to leave.

Getting married will ensure we stay together.

It's perfect.

I can make both my dreams come true.

I take a deep breath and focus on her rich brown eyes, which always make my nerves dissipate. "Lacy, I never thought I'd be so lucky to meet the love of my life in high school—"

"Don't," she cuts me off, placing her palm over the ring, concealing it.

"It's okay," I say with humility. With enough emotions for both of us, I don't hold back. She needs to know how I feel. We'll both remember this proposal for the rest of our lives.

Her eyes grow huge, layering more tears, and she shakes her head back and forth. "Please don't," she squeaks out, as her lips wince into a line of emotional turmoil that don't match any expressions of joy I've ever seen.

In fact, this isn't joy at all!

Her cheeks glow red over her freckles, and she continues to shake her head rapidly. Her top teeth crash down on her bottom lip. Fear slams into my chest so hard, it threatens to knock me over. I grab my chest with my palm and push past the constriction to ask, "Lacey, what's wrong?"

"It's not you," she blurts out a bullet that echoes in all four chambers of my heart.

"It's not me." I force my lips into a smile. "Don't you know that's what people say when they are breaking up with someone?" A nervous chuckle slips from my lips. When a tear slips out of her eye and trails down her cheek, I go frozen. "You're breaking up with me?" I blubber out, all the words jumbling together into one giant word.

This can't be real.

We've never even fought.

I'm down on one knee, holding a diamond ring, and she's breaking up with me!

I blink, waiting for her to respond to the silence she created.

She nods.

"Wait. What?" I drop the ring to my side and jolt to my feet, leveling my gaze with hers, digging into her eyes with intensity. "A nod?" She doesn't say anything, and I go off in a full ramble, "I get a nod. A breakup nod? I don't even get a single-word answer?"

As if mocking me, she nods again. I become unglued, waving my arms like a crazy person. "I've loved you every day for the last four years. I just got down on my knee, ready to beg for your hand in marriage, and all I get is a breakup nod!"

Blinking back at me, her gaze is unwavering.

"What did I do?" I reach for her hip, ready to draw her in close to give her a chance to take it all back.

She's clearly lost her mind.

Or maybe it's a joke?

Please, let it be a joke!

She takes a giant heart-stabbing step back, and I scream, "Why would you do this? Is this because I'm m-moving?" I trip over my words as my breath weakens. When I reopen my mouth to continue, I force myself to speak slower. "You don't have to worry about me moving. I planned for everything to work out. We get married, and you come with—"

"I might be falling for someone *else*." Her reply rings around my head, slamming over and over in my brain like a gong going off. It's enough to make me dizzy.

I tip my head forward, partially because my head is throbbing, but also because I've entered into a stage of disbelief, and I rasp, "How long?"

Her lips move but her words are ghosts. Now she looks frightened with raised brows and her skin blanching paler. "I don't know—"

"Tell the truth," I cut her off as my shock quickly morphs into anger. If there's one thing I hate, it's lying. We've been spending our usual amount of time together, nights after hockey practice and weekends. I haven't even had the inkling of an idea that she may be dating someone else.

"It just happened." She raises an anti-climactic shoulder and then tacks on, "I wasn't looking for anything."

"Who is he?" I demand, this time grabbing her hand, taking a second to scan all her perfect fingers. I've memorized the way her hands look, and having her skin against mine sends a ripple right through my chest that nearly takes my breath away. I squeeze out, "I trusted you." A loud phone vibration rumbles from her pocket. Her eyes shift side to side before she replants her gaze on me, pretending to ignore her phone. "Why don't you answer the phone?" I taunt, as it's all too clear what's going on.

"It's fine." Her hand finds her pocket and slides inside. I assume she's going to silence it and pretend this didn't happen. A fire in my chest says, "I won't be played anymore." With a quick reflex, I reach in her oversized pocket, stealing her phone right from her grip, and yank it out for us both to see the name still blinking on the screen: Blake Anton.

My teammate.

My best friend.

We've played hockey together since we were both in preschool, and we were the only two guys from our high school team to be signed to the NHL. It was a huge victory for our little town, and I was proud to share the spotlight with him. Now, my eyes narrow and nostrils flare as my gaze bounces from his stupid name back to Lacy, the woman I love more than anything.

There's only one thing I want—*revenge.*

My fingers curl into the tightest fists as I vow to stop at nothing until I beat Blake.

He may have won the girl.

But I will beat him in hockey.

I will be more successful and richer than him.

I will win life.

Two

Ruth Miller

Twenty-five Years Later

"This just in," the noon news anchor reports from the little black-and-white TV, which hangs above the long diner counter. The TV has been there since my mother opened this place fifty years ago. Yes, it's far from the big screens they have at Red Barn Kabobs, but that TV might very well be the last working black-and-white TV in all of Mapleton. Despite all the complaints from regulars about the fuzzy lines that scroll up over the picture, I don't have the heart to get rid of it. Call me nostalgic, but I love old things.

And yeah, maybe I have a hard time letting go of the past. So what.

I grab Mrs. Wagner's breakfast ticket and punch in the total amount in the till. One of my ears captures all the ways Mrs. Wagner's tulips are doomed this year because they sprouted too early. My other ear stays attuned to the news. What I hear makes the hairs on the back of my neck stand up straight.

"Billionaire Bill Baker has announced he's bringing an AHL team right here to Mapleton. With the team, he's also announced he's already started construction on a brand-new arena, estimated to be around fifty million dollars. The economic boost Mapleton's set to receive from the construction project alone has the city's vendors buzzing with excitement. We can't wait to welcome this new team, and to top it off, Bill's announced a nationwide scout-free search to recruit for his team. For more information on the recruitment process, interested people can go to the website Granite Ice Hockey—"

"What did he say?" I twist my neck until I can zero in on the screen. I've heard the rumors circulating the diner for months. Mapleton has one of the best gossip mills of any small town, and this little diner is a hub. The thing is, I didn't believe the rumors. It didn't make sense for anyone to put a professional team in such a small town, but I guess it's already in motion. "Granite Ice Hockey," I read the website that flashes on the screen while my heart ticks up a notch. *This might be the answer to my prayers! All the years of hoping Noah gets a better life than I can offer and has a chance to escape this poverty.*

I whip out my pen and pad of paper from my stained server apron and jot it down. My fingers jitter when I reread Granite Ice Hockey. It feels special.

"Oh, that Bill Baker is always up to no good," Mrs. Wagner grumbles over the counter. "What does Mapleton need with a hockey team, anyway?"

"Well, I can't say we need a hockey team, but it would be a phenomenal addition. You know my son Noah has played hockey since he was three. He's eighteen now. His dream is to play in the NHL, but his rank isn't high enough to get signed. I'm praying for it, but I can't help but feel like it's my fault. Being a single mom, I couldn't afford a lot of the opportunities most of these kids have now days. Shoot, half of the time, I couldn't even pay for him to go to open skate at our indoor rink, and he had to practice on the frozen pond."

"I don't know if it's your fault." Her head tilts thoughtfully to the side. "These kids now days think the world revolves around them. It's every little boy's dream to play pro sports.

What most of them need to learn is, they aren't that special. It's better to learn that early, so they can plan on a solid career. Maybe, tell your son, Noah, to try plumbing. You know it's only a two-year program. I hear those guys are always busy. Have you tried to find a plumber lately? You can't hardly get one to call you back." She points her knobby knuckled finger at me, wagging it around as if I'm the one who needs a lesson. "That's a solid income."

Working at a diner, I've heard it all. Living as a single mom, I learned many lessons. Some over and over again. A knot bumbles in my throat as I can't fathom the audacity this woman has to wag her finger at me. I don't need to tell my son to abandon his hopes and dreams.

For what?

To help me run this crummy diner?

I gave up all my dreams to help him build a better life.

I'll be the last person to tell him to give up his dreams.

I take her debit card and close out her ticket. When I hand back her card, I smile as politely as I can. "I'm by no means defending a billionaire, but I'll always help my son chase his dreams. That means I'm beyond happy we're getting a hockey team."

"Ol' Bill can start it, but mark my words, his team is going to be a laughingstock," she says with a huff as she stuffs her card back into her pristine leather wallet. She takes another moment to tuck that perfect leather wallet into her immaculate leather bag and gingerly raises it to her bony shoulder before she turns on her heel and heads out.

My heart pounds so hard, I place my hand over my chest and force myself to take a few deep breaths. Why did I let her get to me like that? Maybe it's time I switch to decaf? My gaze skirts to the side of the counter, where I have my travel mug filled to the brim with coffee. I haven't had more than a few sips out of it, as this morning has been insane.

No, it's not the coffee.

It's living this life where I feel as if I'm being punished for my past—something I didn't even choose. Some cards are just dealt. Poverty isn't for the weak. It's definitely made me strong. If I know one thing, I don't want this life for Noah.

Helping Noah pursue his dream doesn't scare me at all.

What scares me is Noah giving up on his dreams like I did. He has serious talent. He just needs someone to see it and give him a chance.

My gaze drifts back to my pad of paper with the words Granite Ice Hockey on it. I rip the top sheet off, fold it, and slide it in my back pocket. Thanks to that news report, I know exactly who this person is going to be...

The front door to the diner wafts open, and in walks my favorite person. Noah's wearing his Mapleton High School Hockey hoodie, which puts a smile on my face. I haven't seen it since last Saturday. He's one of those sweet boys who has a habit of always lending it to a cute girl at a dance, and then it goes missing for weeks. I wouldn't mind if those hoodies didn't cost me a full day's tips. I forgo a traditional greeting, and say, "You got your hoodie back."

"Yeah, I told you Morgan had it." He pulls out a counter stool and slides one leg over it, while he drops his schoolbag on the empty one next to him.

"And you and Morgan are—"

"Just friends," he cuts me off with a look that warns me not to ask any more about it.

"How did your history exam go?" I grab a bar towel and wipe the counter in a large arc pattern. Not because it needs cleaning. I keep a spotless counter. I have learned Noah tends to open up more if he doesn't feel like I'm hovering. I miss the days when he easily spouted out all the events of his days. I get he must grow up, and it's only normal for him to want some privacy. I'm grateful we are still as close as we are.

"I got seventy-nine percent."

"That's a C, huh?" He doesn't need me to tell him what the grading scale is. My statement is more me thinking through what that percentage will do to his plummeting semester average. It's passing. It will keep him on the high school team, but I worry it won't be enough for college. "Yeah, Cs get degrees, right?"

"Right."

"I also saw your math test grade when I was cleaning off the kitchen counter this morning," I say it gently, but I don't miss the way his shoulders stiffen.

He sighs without looking at me. "I passed."

"Barely," I say, sliding onto the barstool next to him. I don't usually sit when the diner is open. It's important for everything to always look professional. But when it comes to my son, I make sure he knows I'm here. He suffers from serious anxiety and, at times, it's made testing impossible. We've tried so many things over the years to ease the pain he has with his disorder. Nothing has ever really taken it away, although meds seem to help. I've learned not to push.

He gives me that teenage boy shrug. It's one-half defense and the other half I-don't-want-to-talk-about-it. I let the silence hang for a moment. If he wants to talk about it, he will. Clearly, he doesn't, so I move on. "So… I heard something just now on the news. They're bringing in a new hockey team."

That gets his attention. His gaze rises slowly until it locks on mine.

"They're hosting scout-free tryouts." I keep my tone casual but watch him closely.

He gives me an angled look. "Scout free?"

I nod. "Yeah, I guess it's a part of a big push to find the right guys."

His brow furrows, and I see the war already waging behind his eyes. "I don't know if it's worth it to even try. There's no way I'd stand out. Besides, if I was good enough, scouts would already be after me."

I reach out and gently nudge his hand. "No, honey. Not always. Sometimes scouts miss the good guys. You know how it is. It comes down to having the playing time and the right shot. Often, the good people don't get the chance to play when the scouts are watching."

He stares at his hands on top of the counter.

I lean in. "I'm not saying it'll be easy." I don't tell him it might be his only shot out of this poverty cycle. His grades are terrible. Even if he gets into a community college, I'm not sure he has the attention span to do any better than he did in high school. Sure, he can do a trade school. I mean, I guess like Mrs. Wagner said, there's always plumbing, but again, I don't have any money to help him pay for that. He'll be saddled with loans.

Man, I hope for his sake, he sees his potential.

"Noah, I'm being completely honest with you. If I didn't think you had a shot, I wouldn't encourage you. I would never want to set you up for heartbreak, but this is different. This is hockey. You have just as much drive as anyone else. You should try."

The air between us thickens, and he glares at me like if I say one more thing he'll bolt. Then, finally, he lets out a long breath. "So, if I decide to try out, will you come with me?"

I freeze, not from hesitation, but from surprise. My throat tightens because he could've asked anyone. He has tons of friends and guys on his high school team, but he's asking me.

I'm looking at him, but my mind does some weird time warp thing, where all the years fold in on themselves. Every early morning practice. Every late-night ice time. Every extra hot cocoa to comfort a bruised knee. My friends always said, when Noah gets to be a teenager, he won't want me around, but that's not the case. He still wants me here, and it warms my mama heart, making all the sacrifices worth it. I smile, blinking an extra time as I try not to get sappy. "Yeah, if that's what you want. I'll be there."

"Thanks, Mom." Rolling his bottom lip in, his gaze grows distant for a beat.

I slide off the stool and scan the tables. Most of them are empty, as it's before the dinner rush. Noah and I eat early, or I don't get a chance to eat until after I close. "I'm having Margie make me hashbrowns. Should I ask her to make you an omelet?"

"Sure, extra meat for me, please, but don't you know hashbrowns don't count as a meal?"

"You know I prefer to snack." I pull out my pad, scribble out our order and push it through the window. As I turn my focus back to him, his gaze floats above my head. What I wouldn't do to know what he's thinking. He's at the age where he has so many big decisions ahead of him.

So many possibilities.
I want all his dreams to come true.

Three

Bill

I sure didn't expect it to look like this.

Tucked at the edge of the park, the frozen pond looks more like a Hallmark movie set than a tryout rink. White string lights crisscross above the ice. There's even a snack stand with peppermint cocoa and soft pretzels. It's charming, but nothing like the sharp lines and plexiglass of a hockey arena. Since my arena isn't ready yet, this will do.

I can't help imagining what my arena will look like when it's finished. Cushion seats, luxury boxes, a custom Jumbotron, an entire food court. The kind of place kids dream of stepping into someday. I'm halfway through mentally calculating the space in my luxury box when chaos breaks out right in front of me.

"Ah! Sorry! I slipped!" a voice calls from my left, perking my attention to where two kids have knocked over an entire tray of cocoa that a concession worker was carrying. The concession guy is covered in cocoa, and his eyes grow wide with fury or maybe pain as I'm guessing that liquid is hot. Styrofoam cups roll across the packed snow, while napkins flutter away in the light breeze.

I catch a napkin midair and peer at the concession guy, feeling his pain. "Why don't you go ahead and get cleaned up. I can take care of this mess."

"Are you sure?" He gives me an unamused grin.

"Totally, it's my pleasure." I wave him off.

"Thanks, and sorry," he quickly replies as he spins on his heel, heading toward the bathrooms.

"You're welcome," I call after him as I crouch, hurriedly gathering napkins before they blow away. I don't have a bag or anything to throw them into. A fast eye sweep tells me there are no trash cans on this side of the park. I know for a fact there are some garbage cans by the bathrooms, so I stuff the napkins in my deep jacket pockets until I can circle around to the trash cans.

"Here's another one," a voice says, sounding amused and extremely close. I glance up, and a jolt of electricity shoots right through me. A woman is standing behind the railing, bundled in a pink coat with a white beanie that makes the whites of her eyes pop against the dark blue sparkle. Her hair falls in soft curls, and a sparkle of laughter in her gaze hits me square in the chest. She holds out an empty cocoa cup. "I caught one for you."

For me?

I blink.

Does she think I'm the janitor?

I give her a side-eye as I ponder this for a moment. I could correct her. Nobody has ever given me their garbage before, as most people—especially in Mapleton—know exactly who I am. It's sort of funny. I take the cup, and a smile grows on my lips. "Thank you."

She smiles back and turns her attention to the rink. Her side profile is even more beautiful or maybe equally. It's hard to decide, but I find myself mesmerized by her pink lips pinching together like she's nervous.

"Who are you watching?" I don't plan on talking, but I guess my curiosity gets the best of me.

"Number nineteen." She nods toward the ice. "My son."

I follow her gaze.

The kid she's pointing to is flying across the ice. He gets the puck after only a few seconds, and he takes an open shot, missing the goal. Rough. That was an easy shot. The kid has got raw speed, but not much else yet. "He's got wheels," I say, as I don't have the heart to tell her how bad that shot was.

She beams like I've handed her a gold medal. "He's played since he was three. I didn't know anything about the sport. He found an old puck at a yard sale, and the lady gave it to him. He's been obsessed ever since. Hockey's his dream, you know? But the scouts haven't shown any interest in him. I knew when I heard about these tryouts, it was meant to be."

I flick my gaze back to her kid but stay more aware of her than I probably should. There's something in the way she talks about him as her voice fills with pride. Like she's forcing herself to stay positive for him. "He's lucky to have someone who believes in him."

"That I do," she says. "I believe in showing up. Even when it's cold and my toes are numb, I've been at every single game."

"That's dedication."

"I guess it is."

Her hand hovers midair for a second before she tucks a strand of hair behind her ear. "I'm Ruth," she says. "Ruth Miller."

I hesitate for a second too long.

I don't usually have to introduce myself. I get I'm not dressed in my usual clothes, as I'm wearing a plain blue windbreaker and jeans. I don't need her to know who I am for any ego boost, but something about her makes me want to tell her the truth. "Bill," I say finally. "Bill Baker."

She tilts her head, and I count, one second. Two. Then—bam—recognition hits. Her eyes go cartoon-wide.

I smile, bracing for the inevitable wave of awkwardness.

She gasps, a hand flying to her mouth. "Oh no! I handed you garbage!"

Chuckling, I smile wide. "You did."

"I'm *so sorry*," she says quickly. "I thought you were staff. I wanted to do my part to keep the park clean, and I didn't see a trash can!"

"It's okay," I reply, amused. "Honestly? It was kind of nice to have a regular conversation. I don't get too many of those. Most people are too nervous to say much around me."

She groans, covering her mouth with both of her palms as she mutters, "This is so embarrassing!" She turns away from me, as if facing the other direction will make her disappear.

"Don't be embarrassed." I lean in slightly. "You made my night more interesting—"

"Hey, Bill!" One of the organizers is waving me over with a clipboard in hand. "Can you come look at this real quick?"

I sort of want to talk to her more. She's facing away from me, but I can see the back of her cheeks growing rosier by the minute. It's oddly adorable, but regretfully duty calls. "Excuse me, ma'am" I tell her, "I need to check on something."

"Right." She throws up her hand in a wave, still shaken as she's struggling to not look at me.

I step to the side, calling back, "You've got a good kid out there, and he's got a good mom."

She tosses a quick glance over her shoulder, and my chest heats as she holds my gaze for a moment. "Thank you."

I lift the empty cocoa cup in a little salute. "And thanks for the garbage." Then I walk away, fighting the stupid grin that won't leave my face.

The clipboard's waiting for me before I even make it all the way across the ice. Coach Carlson, my head coach, shoves it into my hands like he's handing over a death sentence verdict. "These are the cuts we're thinking of for the first round," he says. "Bad timing, no control. We've got enough talent out here, we don't need to waste time on these kids."

I scan the list. A dozen names. None of them are surprises, but I see #19 Noah Miller on the bottom of the list.

My gut tightens.

I flick my gaze across the ice. Ruth's eyes are locked on the ice like she's willing something magical into existence.

My gaze goes back to Noah.

The kid is fast.

I'll give him that much, but Carlson is correct in his assessment. There are better guys here. Every shot he's taken so far has either gone wide or died on his stick.

Still, there's a niggling in the back of my head, saying to keep him around, to give him a chance to open up a little more. If anything, making the cut will give him an ego boost, which might fuel his adrenaline and help him out. "Hold off on cutting number nineteen," I say, handing the clipboard back by shoving it into his stomach the way he did to me.

Carlson's gaze drops to the board. "Are you serious?"

"Yeah, I agree with you that he's raw, but there's something there. I don't think he's shown us his full potential yet. Let's give him one more round."

"You're the boss." He blows out a breath before pressing his lips together.

My eyes are back on the ice, just as Noah takes a sharp turn. I hold my breath, hoping he shows me what I need, but he loses his balance and wipes out hard, landing flat on his back.

Carlson sees it too, and he groans, "C'mon, Bill. We're wasting our time with that one."

I don't answer because my gaze floats back to his mother. Ruth's expression doesn't crack as she watches her son get right back on his skates.

My chest pulls tight.

Not because of the fall or that kid, but because of her.

There's something about the way she's bracing for disappointment and daring to believe in this dream that tugs at something I thought I'd buried under business plans a long time ago.

I don't know what her story is.

I didn't get where I am today by following the rules and the perfect clipboard plans. I trust my gut. My gut tells me to give this kid a second chance.

Four

RUTH

I'm shivering, and it's not from the cold, though it's definitely seeping in through the seams of my old coat. This is all nerves, curling up like they always do when something feels too good to be true.

Outside the rink, I do my best to scan the crowd. Parents are loitering like me. We all pretend to scroll on our phones, but I don't doubt for a second everyone's ears are attuned to the conversation around them, as we wait for a word of how things go.

Unlucky me, I'm stuck replaying the exact moment I casually handed Bill Baker, the team's owner, trash.

Seriously?

Out of all the possible interactions with a living legend, I went with, "Here, sir, please dispose of this garbage."

I've lived in Mapleton the majority of my life, and I've never had the chance to meet him. How in the universe did it only happen that today, of all days, I casually run into him.

And as if that wasn't enough, I had to double down with an extra dose of humiliation by blabbering about my son like I was on a personal mission to sabotage Noah's chances of making the team.

Shaking my head, I resist the urge to scream or cry or both.

In romance novels, people get these fun little meetups called meet-cutes.

Me? I get meet-garbage.

Bill was nice about it, but he must think I'm looney. And what team owner wants a kid with a looney mom on the team?

And then there was that fall Noah took. He went down hard. Sure, he got right back up like he always does, but it had to be the worst timing because Bill was looking directly at him. I press my lips together, trying not to let the fear take over me as the players start spilling off the ice.

Standing on my toes, I struggle to see around the hordes of people. I knew there was a good turnout, but this is crazy. It's shoulder-to-shoulder people as everyone meanders to find their party.

"Mom," a voice I'd know anywhere slices through the cold air, and I spin on my heel. Noah jogs the last few steps toward me, waving a sheet of paper in his hand like it's a golden ticket. "I made it!" He beams at me with a smile so wide, I take a second glance at it.

For a second, I just blink. "You made the team?"

"Not the team, but I made it to the next round!" He passes the paper to me. "They scheduled me back tomorrow at ten. I have school, but there's no way I can miss this."

My hand goes to my mouth. "Noah, I, uh, I'm speechless, you made it?"

He beams the brightest smile he's had in forever. "I can't believe it, especially since I didn't play that well."

"I believe it," I say, steadying my voice. "They are lucky to get you."

He throws his arms around me, squeezing hard. "Thanks, Mom."

I blink fast, trying not to let tears blur the moment. I sort of want to tell him I met the team owner, and I handed him garbage like an idiot. Maybe it will lighten the mood, but what if Noah gets embarrassed? He doesn't need to know everything I do. Instead of saying something, I hug him back, tightly. "I'm so proud of you."

At a beat, he pulls away and practically runs to the car. I follow behind, still floating somewhere between shock and joy. Inside the car, he takes the driver's seat, talking a mile a minute. It's like he's too hyper to sit still, and he drums his fingers against the steering wheel in rhythm with whatever song is playing faintly through the speakers. His window is cracked enough to let the cold in, pinking his cheeks even more. He's glowing. "I mean, okay, yeah, I fell," he says with a laugh, "but maybe nobody saw that, because they never said anything. That coach, uh, the one in the blue jacket? He gave me this little nod. You know what I mean?"

I smile, trying to mirror his energy, but my stomach knots.

"Did you see that one kid try to cut me off?" Noah continues, animated. "He was fast, but I got around him. The coach definitely noticed how fast I was at that time. You saw that, right?"

"I saw that," I confirm softly. "You're always the fastest guy out there."

His eyebrows hike. "Right? I felt it, you know? Like I belong out there."

My heart lurches, as I can't help but allow it to swell with pride.

This is my son.

He's almost got a shot at his dreams.

It's surreal, and I turn toward the window. The defrosters are on, melting the frost into little rivers across the glass. He's still talking, lost in the thrill of the moment. "Like I don't want to get ahead of myself, but this could be it, right?"

I nod, because it's true.

"And if I make it through this next cut..." He exhales, full of wonder. "Everything could change."

I swallow hard, because he's right.

Everything could change.

My phone buzzes on my lap, and I drop my gaze to see an email notice.

Email: School Counselor – Re: Noah Miller Hockey Eligibility

My stomach sinks before I even open it.

Hi Ms. Miller, I wanted to reach out about Noah's academic standing. His GPA has dropped below the eligibility line for extracurricular participation. Specifically, math is the concern.

In the past, Mr. Brooks allowed retakes if there is a specific reason. However, he's not just going to offer it. We'll need to schedule a meeting to allow Noah to show his seriousness. I'm happy to coordinate with Mr. Brooks (his math teacher).

My chest tightens.

I glance at Noah, who's drumming his fingers against the wheel like he's already imagining his name on a jersey. My heart fractures. I don't think Granite Ice is concerned about his high school GPA, but they will be concerned if he's not holding up his responsibilities and gets kicked off his high school team.

I type back quickly.

Me: Would it be possible to offer extra credit? This is really important to him.

The response comes within a minute.

I understand. Mr. Brooks is known to be somewhat flexible, and he has offered extra credit in the past. I'm looking at his calendar, and his prep time is tomorrow morning at 10:00 AM. He said he can meet with us then.

10:00 AM.

The same time as tryouts.

I freeze, thumb hovering over the screen. My gaze cuts to Noah, who is still happily drumming away. He's never happy. He's been at the peak of his teenage-grumpy years, not to mention he suffers from anxiety that at times is debilitating. I haven't seen him like this in a long time.

Now what do I do?

I stare at the screen as my pulse hammers in my ears. I could make up an excuse tomorrow. Maybe I could tell them we are coming, but then my car didn't start. That way we aren't purposely late, and hopefully Mr. Brooks still sees us.

I hate to lie.

But this is Noah's one shot to play hockey.

But can he really get this shot if he loses his eligibility to play high school hockey? There's only one more game left in their season. If he doesn't get a chance to play after that, what is the point?

I close my eyes, leaning my head back against the seat as stress swirls around my head. Noah isn't the smartest kid. He's clearly intelligent in some things, but I knew since he was a little kid he had a bit of a learning disability that made it hard for him to do math. Sure, he's behind what teachers consider average, but I'm proud he's passing.

Noah chuckles beside me with unfiltered joy. "Did you see me on that last drill? I was flying."

"Yeah," I reply, my voice catching with my eyelids clenched. This is where I miss having a co-parent. Noah's dad was the love of my life. God had other plans for us, taking him when Noah was just a toddler. I hate to think about all the ways we missed out. It's times like these where it would be nice to have someone else I can pull into help. If anything, he could go to the school meeting with Noah, while I ran down to the park to try to explain our situation to Bill.

My head tips to the side as I rewind my thought:

I wonder if I could speak to Bill?

I mean, I know who he is now, and he seems *nice* enough.

Sure, he has hundreds of guys all fighting for the same spot, but he must see something in Noah. There's no way I can possibly be any more embarrassing than I was today.

No.

There's no way that will work.

If I don't show up to school, his math teacher will be upset.

I tip my head the other way, arguing with myself, but he's likely to be upset anyway, and Noah can handle himself.

If I don't try to explain it to Bill, then Noah misses his shot, and the worst Bill can say is no.

I'm not afraid of being told no. I've heard it many times.

I tip my head back the other way, pondering how to explain this all to Noah. He's so insanely happy. At least for the moment, I can't take this from him. I'll tell him in the morning after he has a good night's rest. He'll need all the sleep he can get.

"Hey," he says, cutting into my thoughts. "Is everything okay? You're quiet."

"Everything is great." I force a smile, my voice catching in my throat. "I'm just proud of you and enjoying how happy you are."

Five

BILL

I stand firm in my spot at the far end of the rink, clipboard in hand, headset buzzing with the chatter on the other side. The air's crisp, but the sun shines through clouds in patches, glinting a sheen off the ice. Even with the sunshine, it's not any warmer, and I pull my coat tighter.

"We're all set," Coach's voice crackles in my ear. "The first group of guys is hitting the ice."

"Copy that." I flip the page on my clipboard to find the group one player bios. I've been over these pages so many times, the numbers and names blur together.

Until I catch one that stands out.

#19 – Noah Miller: Local. Fast. Inconsistent puck handling.

That's the kid who fell right in front of me during the final drill, but his speed was undeniable. My eyes lift from the clipboard and scan the ice.

Players are warming up, and pucks are already banging against the boards. I take roll call in my head: #22, #1, #8...but no #19. "Hey, guys, anyone got eyes on nineteen?" I ask into the mic.

"Not on the bench," Coach replies. "Might be a scratch."

Strange.

I read his bio again.

Local kid. No travel barrier. The weather is cold, but the roads should be clear, so that's not an excuse. I frown but shift my attention back to the drills as the first shooter, #12, takes his shot.

It's smooth.

Then another. And another.

I glance down. #12 – Axl Erikson. Nebraska.

"Boy, that kid from the Midwest's got hands," I say into the mic as I'm already marking a check next to his name.

"He's a lock," Coach says, sounding satisfied. "No question about that one. If we don't grab him, someone else will."

I nod, about to make a note about his speed when "Excuse me!" a voice calls out from behind me.

I ignore it, thinking it's not for me.

"Hi! Sorry! Uh—hellooooo?" The voice is getting closer.

I press my earpiece tighter, trying to hear the guys as this person is now next to me and is being awfully loud.

"Hey, Mr. Baker?" the voice continues, and I turn slowly, already bracing myself to be irritated. When I glance up, my breath stalls.

It's Ruth from yesterday. That kid's mother. She's wearing the same beanie on her head, and her cheeks are flushed pink to match her coat. She's grinning, but it's the kind of smile people wear when they're faking a good day.

Before I have a chance to say anything, she exhales in a rush. "Yes. Hi. I'm sorry to interrupt you. I know you are very busy with super important things like running this team, and this is not the time, but, uh, I must talk to you about my son, number nineteen."

I lower my clipboard, half-annoyed, but my curiosity is certainly piqued. "He's not on the ice."

"I know. He's had a school thing." Her words cut off all choppy, like she's already choking back tears. "He's eighteen, but still in high school, and he got called into a meeting about his grades. It was the only time he could meet with the teacher and the counselor. I couldn't move it, so I, uh, told him I moved the tryout."

I squint. "You what?"

"I told him I talked to you, and you agreed to move it to later," she says, her cheeks fluster into a deeper shade of red. "I didn't want him to miss the school meeting, and I didn't want him to panic, because he has a serious anxiety disorder. Once he has a panic attack, it's over. Okay, I know how that sounds. I do. But I needed him to go to the school, because if he doesn't get his grades up, he's not eligible to play anywhere. Shoot, he might not even graduate. And I have worked too many night shifts at the diner to have him not graduate. So, failing math isn't an option. And I thought maybe I could somehow ask very nicely..." Her words fall off, and she stares at me, batting these thick lashes that make me double take.

"Let me get this straight," I say slowly, as I'm more en-tertained at this point than I'm annoyed. "You assumed you could reschedule a professional team tryout?"

She winces. "When you put it like that, it sounds so rude, but yes, sort of. But also, I didn't really assume. Assume is such an imposing word. I will assure you; I don't want to be an imposition to you. I'm more than happy to find a way to make this up. I wasn't assuming anything. It was definitely a hope and a prayer situation more than an assumption."

There's a beat of silence.

Then, involuntarily, I huff out a laugh. I get he is her son, but that isn't fair to the guys who were here on time. They all had other stuff to do too, but they made my team a priority, as they should if they want to work for me.

Her eyes dart up. "Why are you laughing?"

"This is crazy." I'm unable to help the smile tugging at the corner of my mouth.

Going on, her voice cracks. "I don't want him to lose everything before he ever gets a real chance. He's been dreaming about this since he was three. Frankly, I've given up all my hopes and dreams for this. Can you please consider staying late? I'll pay for your time." She starts to reach for her worn purse slung over her shoulder, and that's when I stop her.

"Look, ma'am." I hold out my hand, stopping her from digging in her purse.

"You can call me Ruth."

"Ruth." I shift awkwardly, my fingers curling around the clipboard like it might shield me from how wrecked she looks. "You must understand how these things work. We need guys who can make this team their priority. If they can't make it to their tryout, that's a big sign about their loyalty."

"I—I'm not saying he has to make the team, but he was so happy yesterday," she stammers. "I messed this up, but can you at least pretend to let him try out?"

Before I can even respond, my headset crackles. "Bill, we need you down by the benches now."

I glance over my shoulder, where everyone's in a huddle, and then back at Ruth. "I have to go," I tell her as my regret slips in.

She holds up her hand in a nonmoving wave. "Of course. Thank you for your time."

I head down to the huddle, where the stats are being reviewed. It's not as tough of a cut this time, because there are a few clear standouts. As the last whistle blows, I'm confident in the list of guys we've kept this round.

Amid the bustle, a small table has been set up where final decisions are being handed out. One by one, players approach with tension visible on their faces. Coach Carlson hands each skater a sheet of paper. For some, the news is disappointing. I offer a firm handshake to everyone and try to encourage them to continue to work hard. When Axl, my top pick, comes to the front of the group, the tone shifts. I reach out to shake his hand with enthusiasm. "Well done," I say. "See you back here next weekend."

"Thanks, sir." He shakes my hand and sidesteps out of the way. That's when something catches my gaze in my peripheral vision.

Ruth.

And jogging up to meet her in full gear, with his helmet under his arm, is her son, Noah. She turns to look at him with a frown and shakes her head, clearly saying something like *it's too late.*

She doesn't see me watching.

And something in me gives.

I don't know what to call it. I'm not exactly the type of guy to hand out anything. I didn't get where I am by getting pity. I find myself lifting my hand and calling across the ice, "Number nineteen! Glad you could finally make it. Let's see what you've got."

Ruth whips her head around, and her eyes pop wide.

And me?

I already know I'm in trouble. I don't see the point in carrying this out any longer. The guy isn't good enough. He'll be heartbroken in thirty minutes, but at least he'll be mad at me and not his sweet mom. She seems to have enough guilt.

Not that I care about her guilt.

Call it my good deed for this decade.

Noah heads to the ice, and I speak into the headset. "Coach, we have one more tryout. Can you head to the ice and let him run a drill?" I barely turn my gaze that way, and footsteps crunch in the snow coming from the other direction. What do you know, Ruth is standing a few feet away from me, her arms crossed, most likely from the cold, but her eyes eagerly search for mine.

To be honest, the woman looks exhausted. Not like she got a bad night's sleep, but from the kind of tired that piles up over a long time. "Hey," she says quietly.

I nod only once. "Hey."

She shifts her weight from one foot to the other. "I want to say thank you. We both know you didn't want to do that, but I appreciate it." Her voice is sweet, but there's no mistaking the weight behind her words.

"You don't need to thank me." I fix my focus back on the ice. Noah's skating super-fast again. Lucky for him, this time he hasn't wiped out yet.

A beat passes, and she goes on, "I'd like to repay you somehow."

I shake my head. "That's not necessary."

She lets out a breath. It's like someone who's had to accept help more times than she'd like and is clenching to the last piece of pride. "I know it's not much, but I've got a little diner, just down the road," she says, quieter now. "It's nothing special, but I'd love for you to stop by sometime when you're hungry, and it's on the house."

I arch a brow. "Thanks for the offer, but that's quite all right. I'm not exactly hurting for a meal."

She smiles at that, but then her lips flatten. "I get it. You have better places to go." She pauses, before adding with conviction, "We make a pretty decent stack of pancakes."

"Pancakes?" I echo, as it's starting to become clear this woman doesn't ever give up on anything easily. First it was all about her son. Now it's about her pancakes. She sure is tenacious. "Is that right?"

"They won the blue ribbon in five counties."

I let myself smile at her now. I've finally figured her out. She's not taking no for an answer. "Well," I say, "I can't say no to pancakes. I might try to get over there."

I wait for her to come back with something else she needs me to do for her, but she's quiet, and we stand still for a moment.

"Thank you again." She nods once before she turns and strides back the way she came. With the early morning sunlight casting on her rosy cheeks, the day suddenly feels warmer than it did before. My eyes lock on her as she finds her spot back on the other side of the rink. When I finally focus back on Noah, I'm not wondering when he's going to wipe out again.

Instead, I wonder if pancakes sound good for dinner.

Six

Ruth

A forecasted snowstorm is making the diner eerily quiet. Lately it seems like no matter what I do, I can't get ahead. Business overall is slow. I'm pinching every penny I can to keep this place profitable. I'm lucky to have a slew of regulars who come in the mornings, but my nights have died off.

Except for two regulars, who are night-shift nurses drinking their coffee before their shift starts, the place is empty. Hating to sit because it makes me tired, I stay busy wiping syrup and ketchup off the menus, but my eyes flick to the clock on the wall every few minutes.

I'm not a big caffeine-in-the-afternoon person, but this might be one of those rare nights I make an exception to get through this shift. I turn toward the coffee maker, grab a cup, and fill it with the fresh coffee as the bell on the door jingles.

The hairs on the back of my neck alert, and I feel his presence in the air. Bill Baker saunters in, wearing the same blue windbreaker he wore at the park. He's got an easy stride as he glances around the place, and I find myself smoothing my apron. "You came," I say, trying to sound calm and not wildly out of my comfort zone.

Sure, I invited him.

I didn't exactly expect a billionaire to show up at my humble table.

He bends his lips into a full smile. It's genuine but does little to put me at ease. "You didn't think I would?"

I force myself to match his smile, but my heart is somewhere between my throat and my stomach, bouncing around like it has no idea where it belongs. Noah got done with his practice, and they dismissed him, but neither the coach nor Bill gave him any feedback. They simply said thanks for trying out. It was an odd exchange. Of course, Noah looked disappointed. Since I had to close tonight, I couldn't stay home to find out more. I'm still grateful Bill allowed him that chance. I figured since he wasn't asked to return, Bill wouldn't bother with my pancakes.

I shrug, my lips twitching. "I thought you might be too busy."

"I am busy," he says, "But I still have to eat, and someone promised me the best pancakes. And honestly, that kind of boldness demands a follow-through."

I sputter out a laugh before I stop myself. My nerves unravel a bit more as I start to understand his sense of humor. I find a real smile. "Well, you are in luck. The griddle is warm, and no one else is in line. You can take any seat you want."

He picks a stool at the counter, sliding on it with the kind of ease that my regulars do.

I hand him one of the clean menus I just wiped off. "Do you drink coffee?"

"Not usually, but if you think I need one, I'll try one."

"I see how you are." I pour him a cup and slide it over. He doesn't hesitate to lift it to his lips and take a sip.

He pushes the menu back at me without looking at it. "You said I must try the pancakes, so that's what I will have. And if you've got real maple syrup, I might have to make that a double stack."

"Of course I do." I write his order on a ticket and push it through the window for Margie to grab. Then I turn back, he's staring at the photo wall next to him. When my mom ran this diner, she used to collect photos of the locals and hang them up. That was many years ago. Most of them are black-and-white Polaroids of everything from the 4th of July parade to the Little League teams we've sponsored over the years. If I had to bet, the majority of the people in those photos are long since passed, as my mom herself has. That was her community, and I never had the heart to remove the photos. They remind me of my mom and her love of the community. Aside from our pancakes, this diner is also a well-known for our photo wall.

"Is that Brad Wilson?" Bill points to a photo of a young boy, maybe sixteen years old. He's skinny as a pole and standing in front of a busted-up pickup.

I step forward, even though I've looked at this photo so many times I've memorized it. "Yeah, he used to come in here with his mom, who was friends with my mom. He was a few years older than me in school, but I didn't know him. Did you know him?"

"Yeah, I knew him and still do. He hunts with my cousin," Bill says, squinting. "He has that deep purple scar on his neck. Look, you can even see it in this photo"

"I see it." I nod. "Interesting that you know him. What a small world."

"It is a small world, especially here in Mapleton. Have you lived here your whole life?" he asks, sipping his coffee.

"Born and raised." I tuck a hair behind my ear, but my hand pauses on top of my head where my hair feels a tad greasier than I'd prefer. In the bustle of the day, I didn't have time to wash it, and I threw it back in a ponytail.

Oh, big regret now.

Why didn't I shower?

Bill's gazing at me as if expecting me to expand on my thought, so I rush out, "I left for a bit after I graduated high school. I had this dream to see the world, but that didn't last long."

He tilts his head. "Oh really? How come?"

I shrug, drifting my focus back to the wall. I understand why the regulars love these photos so much. It makes for an easy place to gaze. "Oh, you know. Life was leading back. I had gotten married and pregnant, which were good things. Then unexpectantly I ended up being a single mom. I tried, but I couldn't do it alone. I didn't have an education and was barely making any money and had to pay for daycare. My mom offered me a chance to come back and help her run this place. Since she was grandma, she sure didn't mind when I brought Noah with me to work nights. Many times on her nights off, she watched him for me. It saved me a lot of money on childcare. Plus, we enjoyed working together. What about you? Are you originally from here?"

His brow lifts. "Yeah, I grew up on the other side of the tracks. Right near that old railroad bridge."

"Are you talking about the one off Main Street they're getting ready to tear down this spring?"

"That's the one." He chuckles until the lines by his eyes crease. "I always thought that old bridge would crumble any day. I guess the city finally got sick of waiting for it to self-destruct. It's been through a lot. We used to jump off it as kids. Shoot, as fearless as I was back then, I didn't tell anyone I actually peed my pants a little the first time I jumped."

I laugh from my belly because I know the exact sensations, but I also wasn't expecting Bill to open up about something like that. "We did that too. I only jumped once though. That was enough for me. Always a collector of things, I preferred to catch the fireflies. Did you ever see how thick they were at night?"

His smile softens. "Actually, I didn't get over there much at night. My parents never let me run after dark, but the few times I accidentally stayed late, I noticed that. It was sort of magical the way they appeared, wasn't it?"

"Yeah, it was." For a second, we sit with the memory. Then I add, "It's crazy we never saw each other. What year did you graduate?"

"Oh, I'm old. I graduated last century," he teases. "In the 1900s"

"So old." I chuckle, enjoying his humor. "I was there too. Boy, does that feel like another lifetime ago."

He leans back, gaze still on me. "Sometimes it does, but sometimes it seems like yesterday."

"I haven't thought about that bridge in years. Isn't that funny? All the memories that stay with you, but you don't think about them much."

"Yeah." His lashes lower, hooding the spark in his eyes for a moment. "Even when everything else changes. All the neighborhoods have grown, but that bridge is the same."

"Order's up!" Margie calls as she slides his plate through the window. I turn, grabbing it and his ticket. "As promised, the best pancakes on this side of Vermont." I slide the plate across the counter. With my free hand, I fold his ticket in half and tuck it in my apron pocket.

"I'll be the judge of that." He gives me a teasing smile while unfolding a napkin and leaning forward, fork in hand."

I stand back, watching as he cuts a piece of the pancake with the side of his fork, stabs it, and drops it into his mouth. He maintains a straight expression as he chews. Something tells me he does that to tease me because there's no way he doesn't love it. "Well?" I ask after his chewing has gone on for an insane amount of time.

"Don't know yet. I don't judge off first bites." He returns his fork to his pancake for another bite. "I have to eat the whole thing to make sure the taste is consistent."

"That's fair."

He drops another piece into his mouth. After he swallows it, he looks over at me and says, "About the tryouts, you know, we already had our list of guys we wanted to make the next round before Noah showed up."

My heart catches, squeezing tight. I hadn't expected him to bring that up. I could apologize again, but I already did that. Sorry only goes so far. I honestly struggle to say anything. When I don't, he goes on, "Technically, he missed the tryout. So, Coach Carlson dismissed him when he was done working with him."

"Right," I say, voice coming out small. "I, uh—"

He waves my defense off, speaking over me, "I didn't know what to do with him, but if he can be back next Saturday, we'll run some drills. I'd like to see him on the ice with the other guys. It wasn't really a fair assessment by himself."

I stare at him, stunned as hot tears prick the backs of my eyes.

I didn't expect this.

I'm certainly not going to say no. Noah's one step closer to his dreams coming true, and I want that so much for him. Thank you doesn't sound like it's enough, so instead I say, "This means everything."

"I know it does. I remember when I was his age. My only goal was to play hockey. The thing is, he's got some good qualities. Mainly his speed, but he needs some polishing. I'm hoping if he gets a little push, we'll see more out of him."

I swallow the lump in my throat. That doesn't exactly sound like he's on the team. With so many guys fighting for spots, it's a long shot. Everything has been working out so far. I'm not giving up. Before I know it, he scoops up the last of his pancakes, glances at his watch, and sighs like he's not ready. He smiles at me as he sets his napkin in the center of his plate. "You were right. These were the best pancakes I've ever had, but it's only partially because of the taste."

My head tilts as I'm not quite sure what he means about only partially, but I'm too afraid to ask for clarification. "I'm glad you enjoyed them," I say, but it comes out more breath than voice. "You're welcome back anytime."

"You know something. I'm glad I stopped by. It was nice getting to visit with you." He lingers for a second. Something flickers in his eyes. It's tender, and maybe a little tentative. He gives me a last, quiet smile and walks out.

The bell jingles as the door floats to shut behind him. I stand still with my heart thundering in my chest. That man holds my son's future in the palms of his hands.

Please be good to him, I pray.

Seven

Bill

Snow blows vertically into the rink, like its mission is to bury us all. It's not that light and fluffy snow either. This stuff is hardened into ice pebbles that pelt the side of my face. With my hood cinched up tight, I huddle on the outside of the rink and wait for tryouts to start. My honest assessment: it doesn't look good. My boots are so snow crusted I can't even tell what color they are. I mean, they're black, but I can only say that because I saw the color when I put them on. Now, they are completely white.

Coach Carlson tugs on his scarf, pulling it tighter around his face as he yells over the wind. "This is miserable. Do you want to call it?"

Glancing across the rink, I see a full sheet of the best guys fighting for a spot on my team. Most of them are from out of town, flying in from every state from Maine to California. I know for a fact some of these guys could easily have full-ride college deals, but they are risking it for a chance to be here. Rubbing my hands together, it only takes a minute before I give up and reach in my pockets for my gloves. This is no joke, but I shake my head. "We can't quit. Most of these guys spent hours traveling, so we're giving them a tryout."

Carlson shrugs as his gaze shifts back to the ice. "Your call."

I step closer with my clipboard tucked under my arm. The guys are unstoppable, pushing hard despite the blizzard. I like that. It shows their work ethic.

I start jotting notes.

#9—*Keeps head up, Tracks puck.*

#65—*Battles hard. Doesn't back down.*

Then I hear it, even though the wind is howling. Some cocky kid chirps. I fix my gaze on him. #20. "Might as well send him home now," I mumble as I scratch his number off the list. I don't care how good he is. Mouthy guys poison the locker room. I've seen it. I'm not doing that. If he's mouthy when he's not even on the team, I can't imagine how much his head will inflate once he gets picked.

The wind kicks up, sending the snow pebbles pinging into the side of my face even harder, and I cringe. This is brutal. Within seconds, visibility drops to about ten feet in front of me, and I can't see the center of the rink. On cue, Carlson retrieves his phone, checking the weather app. He turns to me with even more seriousness this time. "The wind chill reading has dropped. They're shutting roads. The county will have a travel ban by nightfall."

Having just begun, I don't want to hear it. There are so many skills I need to see from these guys. This is arguably the most important day for my team. If I don't get the lineup perfect, nothing else matters. I could reschedule but that sounds like a logistical nightmare.

I stare at the guys skating in disordered circles, refusing to quit.

That's when it happens: two guys collide at full speed right in front of me and land smack on their backs. I can't say I blame them because I can barely see either. I hold my breath for a moment as they scramble back up. They seem to be okay for now. I hate to admit it, but it's not worth hurting the guys. I'm going to need them. "Never mind," I grumble to Carlson as I drop my clipboard to my side in frustration. The paper's soaked, and the ink all bleeds together. It's pointless. "I'm over this. Get them off the ice before someone gets hurt."

He blows the whistle and steps onto the ice, yelling, "All right, boys! Off the ice! That's not a request!"

They start funneling off and huddle around us as they seem confused as to what to do next.

I don't know what to do with them.

I wait till they're gathered by the benches with their helmets off. All their faces are bright red. Then I say with heavy disappointment in my voice, "Due to the weather, we're ending tryouts. I can't think straight right now to make final decisions. We'll be reviewing the notes we have over the next few days, and you'll each get a call one way or the other." I step back, but I wobble from the force of the wind. The storm's not letting up, and I can feel the cold working its roots into my bones. Some of the guys' families step forward to collect each other, and they linger near the edge of the rink shivering.

A voice cuts through the air, "Hey, it looks like they just shut down the interstate. If anyone's stuck or needs to wait out the storm somewhere before you can travel, my diner is just up the road, next to that truck stop off the interstate. I'll have hot chocolate and coffee on the house."

I turn toward the voice, but I already know it's Ruth.

She's wrapped in a giant fleece blanket that I don't doubt covers a full-sized coat. Her regular white beanie is encapsulated with snow, but her eyes are bright. I don't know what it is about her. If I were her, I'd go home. Instead, she volunteers her place to host my guys. It's like she's immune to chaos, and I can't help but smirk.

She catches me staring, smiles my way, and calls right at me, "You're welcome to come too, if you aren't busy."

I blink. I wasn't expecting that. People don't usually invite the boss to hang out. My cheeks heat as I ponder how sweet that is of her. "I, uh." I look at Carlson. We've got more than enough work to do, since we must plan an entire roster from only the notes we already have.

Carlson smirks and claps me on the back. "Screw it. We'll go over the roster later. Cocoa sounds like team building to me."

I chuckle, shaking my head. "Yeah. Team building."

We follow the crowd toward the street, Ruth leading the pack as she gives several people instructions on how to get to her place.

The snow keeps hammering the side of my face, and I won't argue a warm beverage sounds amazing.

We do our best to brush the snow from our coats and stomp slush off our boots before we enter Ruth's Diner. By the time

I get there, players and parents cram into booths, and they sip out of mismatched steaming mugs. It's loud, as everyone seems to have something to say all at once. The blizzard is still hammering Mapleton on the outside, but here, it's cozy.

I slide onto the same counter stool I sat on the other day. I like it here, where I get a view of the entire place. Coach Carlson grabs the stool next to me. It's only a second later, and Ruth pops up on the other side of the counter with a full smile on her face. "Coffee, cocoa, or tea?"

"Cocoa," we say at the same time. She disappears into the kitchen and reappears with two blue mugs, setting them in front of us. The only word that slips out of her mouth is, "Enjoy," but the smile on her lips pins my gaze to her as she floats back around the counter with the coffeepot, refilling mugs as she passes through the long narrow aisle.

"Uh, oh," Carlson mutters as he peers over the rim of his mug. "I think she uses real cream."

"Are you allergic?" I half-smile, because I'm only half-listening. I'm too busy watching Ruth buzz around, talking to everyone like they are all her best friends.

"No, not allergic. More like obsessed." He chuckles as he takes a sip and exhales slowly when he lowers the mug back to the counter. "I have a new addiction."

I recognize Noah behind the counter. He's still wearing his practice jersey, but I can't help but notice how he pitches in, helping his mom by grabbing the plates out of the window like he's done this a few times. It's sort of nice to see a young kid working so hard.

Then I hear it behind me:

"Did you see that wrister I put top shelf?" a loud voice booms from across the room, clearly bragging, which I hate. Maybe he didn't realize I'm sitting within earshot, but he needs to learn to shut his mouth if he's going to be on my team. I can't stand cocky guys.

Another kid chimes in, "I deked two guys on that last drill. They went flying in the other direction."

Laughter erupts, and I toss a glance over my shoulder to the round table in the corner. I like confidence, but in my opinion their confidence is a little too loud. I make a mental note. *#5, #41, #88. Cocky with egos.*

Maybe they're good.

Shoot, they might even be great.

I'm not building a calendar of pretty boys. I want to fill my locker room with guys who have the maturity to know when to shut their traps.

Almost instantly, my eyes drift back to Noah serving cocoa. That's the kid who was fast but struggles with his stick-handling. He's sure quiet, and a tad small. He did wipe out, but he got right back up. The best thing is, he keeps his mouth shut and gets to work.

A little girl at the booth directly across from me erupts in a wailing cry like she's hurt. She's probably a sibling to one of these guys. Noah's behind the counter again, and his gaze skips right over me to the kid's mom. "Is she okay?"

"She's fine"—the mom sighs—"just crabby. It's been a long week for her. We couldn't get flights, so we drove from Texas in two days."

One corner of Noah's lips curls up into a thoughtful smile before he disappears back into the kitchen again. I sip out of my cup, noting this is the best hot cocoa I've ever had. Agreeing with Carlson, it's because it's made with real cream. Noah reappears with a fleece blanket draped over one arm, and he walks it over to the little girl, handing it to the mom.

"Here, I totally know how she feels, so much so that I leave this blanket in the office for when I need a nap," he says, not even waiting for a thank you before heading back behind the counter. I watch with wide eyes as the mom wraps the child in the blanket, and she snuggles into her mom. The child is instantly soothed.

Something about it hits me right in the chest. It wasn't about the blanket at all.

Kindness when no one asked for it.

That's something you don't see very often with these young kids.

Carlson leans over, nudging me with his elbow. "Something wrong? You're staring at that kid."

"He's a good kid," I murmur.

Ruth appears by my side with her coffeepot. "Everything okay here?"

"Everything is fine. Thank you." I smirk. "I'm enjoying seeing what the guys are like when they don't think anyone is paying attention."

She parks her free hand on her hip and arches a brow toward the table in the back with the bragging guys. "Yeah, isn't that scary sometimes?"

I laugh at that. She's in a good mood with a full smile on her face, making her easy to talk to. "You seem to be handling the storm and the chaos well though," I say, leaning back.

"It's been one of the best days ever." She blows out an even breath. "Some people just see the storm, but I got to see my son try out for his dream team. It's a crazy surreal feeling, and I guess I owe it all to you. Thank you."

"Don't thank me," I reply. "I'm not giving you anything. I'm doing a job. You're the one who should be thanked, because you opened your restaurant to a whole team of frozen guys with no place to go."

"No need to thank me." Her eyes linger on mine a beat too long. "They looked like they needed it after standing outside."

Before I can reply, someone calls her from the kitchen. She's off again, moving with that same bright energy.

"Well," I say to Carlson as I finish my cocoa. "I need to take off. I'll be calling you after I have time to review these notes.

Let's get this roster set by tomorrow." He nods while sipping from his mug. I slide my wallet out and remove a few hundred dollar bills. When she's not looking, I slip the bills on the cash register where she won't see them until later. There's no way she should be expected to absorb the cost for all these players. Then I sling my coat over my shoulder, not bothering to put it on since I parked right out front, and left my SUV running to keep it warm. I leave without saying goodbye to anyone. There's so much on my mind, I struggle to keep all the guys straight in my head. As the cold air slaps me back into focus, one thought hits me a little louder than the others.

I want Noah on my team.

He's quiet and still a little raw, but his work ethic is there. He's also full of something this sport doesn't always value enough: heart. I mean, what teenager would care to bring a toddler a blanket?

As I pull out of the parking lot, I know I have my first pick.

Eight

Ruth

The last mug clicks the dish rack, and I push it into the automatic washer with a deep breath. With chairs flipped onto tables while the freshly mopped floor dries, I'm finally ready to close. Outside, the snow continues but is easing up. There's a tad more visibility, and the snowplow cleaned the street about an hour ago, so I'm not nervous about getting home. I sent Noah home a couple of hours ago, right after the hockey rush cleared out. I love when he helps me, but I limit how much I use him because he has enough on his plate with school and hockey.

I turn off the lights, one by one, and just before the last light goes out, the door jingles. Without looking, I call out, "Sorry! We're closed."

"Not here to eat. I forgot my wallet," a voice calls out, and I instantly freeze. I found a wallet.

Bill Baker's wallet to be exact.

It was right next to my cash register where there was five hundred dollars in cash. "Oh, hey," I say, softer now that I know it's him. "I set it underneath the till, along with the cash you left me. It's all back where it belongs, inside your wallet."

He takes a step forward, brushing snow from his sleeves. "Sorry, I didn't mean to trouble you."

"No trouble," I say, reaching for it. "I would have tried to call you, but it was nonstop all night, and besides, I didn't have a number..."

He shrugs like it doesn't matter, stepping closer. "It's fine. I just didn't want it sitting here all night."

I hold it out and he takes it, our fingertips brush for a second, which gives me a pause as I ponder if he meant to do that. "I really want you to have the money. I know you offered the drinks on the house, but you had great service, and I'm happy to pay for it. It was a wonderful evening." He slides the bills out of his wallet and tucks them behind the cash register with a stern look on his face, but a teasing gleam in his eye. "Don't make me hide this in your freezer somewhere where it will only get lost."

I chuckle and decide to drop it. It's a sweet gesture for him to pay. He can surely afford it, and I appreciate it. "Well, thank you."

"The roads are terrible," he says, tucking the wallet into his coat. "Do you have a long drive ahead of you?"

I lean back against the counter. "No, I don't live far. Besides, it's not the first time I've ridden out a storm here."

"I guess it's not the worst place. You won't go hungry."

"No." I politely chuckle again.

"Well, thank you again for hosting everyone," he adds, his voice quieter now. "I appreciate it."

"It was my pleasure," I say, feeling like we've already had this conversation earlier, but I go on. "I figured someone had to house them or they'd have frozen in that park."

We linger as the silence stretches. Not uncomfortable exactly, but it doesn't seem like he's in a rush to leave. Suddenly, I'm not in a hurry to leave either. "Are you ready for another stack of pancakes?" I offer, immediately surprised at myself. "Griddle's off, but it doesn't take long to heat up."

He smiles a little. "Tempting, but I just need my wallet, and you need to get home where it's warm and safe."

"Right," I say, brushing my hands on my apron, though they're already clean. "Of course."

He shifts his weight, eyes still on me. "You know, I was watching your son help you tonight, and I have to say you raised a good kid."

I nod, as Noah's my favorite topic to talk about. "Well, I'm biased, but I think he's a good one too. I don't know what I'd do without him."

He pauses for a beat before saying, a little shy but clearly excited, "Hey, the storm's supposed to stop tonight, and I was thinking about going for a drive to see that old bridge again before they tear it down. I'd like to get some photos of it. I was wondering if you'd want to ride along?"

I blink. He's smiling very genuinely, not flirtatiously, but my stomach still twists.

I don't date.

Not like I only go out on first dates.

Like I haven't gone anywhere with anyone since Noah's dad.

Two hearts died the day Noah's dad passed, but only one actually stopped beating. I have Noah, and we've made a nice life together, despite all the immense heartaches. I have no desire to change anything.

But this doesn't sound like a date.

It sounds like he's trying to pay me back for my hospitality, which I don't expect.

My eyes shift side to side as another thought pops in my head—or is this some sort of test?

Like he is trying to see if I'd create a conflict of interest for his team? My palms start to sweat just thinking about it. I don't think it's wise for me to hang out with him, considering he holds Noah's fate in the palm of his hands.

But he's still smiling.

Like this matters to him for a reason he hasn't said yet. I hate to ever say no to people when they need help. Maybe there's a reason he needs to run over there? Against my better judgment, I hear myself slur, "Suuuure."

He beams as he takes a few steps backward toward the exit. "Great. I won't hold you up any longer, because it's late, but I'll text you tomorrow once I make sure the roads are good."

He starts to spin on his heel to walk away, but I blurt out, "Want my number?"

He shakes his head, grinning. "I can grab it from Noah's file."

And just like that, I'm reminded again, even though I didn't exactly forget that this isn't a good idea.

What am I getting into?

Before I can ask for further clarification, he's waving a casual good night over his shoulder.

I stand there watching him go, a little breathless and a little terrified of what I've agreed to.

Anxiety bubbles in my gut, and my gaze slams back to the kitchen counter, where I have a bag of popcorn hidden. I'm going to need a snack while I think about it.

When I arrive home, the house is silent except for the low murmur of a sports commentator echoing from down the hall. I slip off my boots, brush snow from my coat, and pad down the hall toward Noah's room. His door is slightly open. I pause outside, watching him for a moment.

He's reclined on his bed, scrolling on his phone. His expression is focused. In moments like these, he looks older than he is. He's so serious and grown-up. *Where did the time go?*

I don't even realize I've sighed until he glances up. "Hey, Mom, were the roads okay?"

"Yeah." I take a step into his room. "They plowed right after you left."

He holds up his phone. "No word about Granite Ice yet. He never said when he'd get back to us. I'm assuming it takes a while, but I'm getting nervous."

I swallow. "I saw Bill after you left"

Noah raises an eyebrow. "Bill Baker?"

"Yeah, he left his wallet at the diner and came back to grab it, and we spoke briefly," I say quickly. I stop myself before I blurt out anything more.

Like *he asked me to go somewhere.*

Like *I said yes.*

I run a hand through my hair, trying to sort through the noise in my head.

Besides, he was probably nice since I returned his money to his wallet without stealing his credit cards and his identity. So many people would love to get their hands on Bill's wallet.

That's all.

He won't text.

Noah tilts his head. "You look worried. Is everything okay?"

"I'm fine." I force a smile. "I'm excited about your tryout, and I'm really proud of you."

His eyes soften. "Thanks, Mom."

"Say, you never said how the meeting with your math teacher went today."

"It was cringe." He sighs as he dramatically drops his back against his headboard. "But he said I can take a retest exam on Monday. He said he can't drop my first grade, but we can average them together, and that should help bring my grade back over failing."

"Wonderful." I raise an eyebrow. "Shouldn't you be studying for that, then?"

He grins, sheepish as he drops his phone next to him on the bedspread. "I guess."

I step back toward the hall. "I'll leave you to it, then. Try not to spend *all* night watching highlight reels."

"Can't make any promises."

I shake my head, smiling as I turn and call back, "Love you, and I'm headed for bed. I have to be back at the diner to open it."

"Love you too," he calls back.

And as I stroll toward my room, I can't help but think about my date with Bill.

It's not a date! But that doesn't stop the flutter in my chest.

Nine

Bill

Ruth is outside waiting when I pull up to the curb in front of the diner. The moment I see her, something tugs in my gut. I still as she strides forward. She's wearing her pink coat, cinched tight at her waist, and a few wisps of hair blow freely from underneath her white beanie. They frame her face in a way that makes it hard to look away. She steps into my SUV without hesitation, the scent of her, something faintly sweet, curls into the warm air between us.

"So," she says, closing the door with a solid click. Her eyes are bright as she takes a moment to buckle her seat belt. "This is exciting. It's been a while since I've been down that highway. I'm assuming you checked the road report?"

I clear my throat and force myself to focus on operating my car and not staring at her. "I just looked." My voice is rougher than I expected. "Everything should be fine."

"I'm happy to see it again, and a little sad to know it's the last time," she says softly. "It was thoughtful of you to ask me to come with you."

I exhale as I ease my SUV out of the parking lot. "I'm glad you said that. At first, I thought I was being silly to care so much about an old bridge, but when I couldn't stop thinking about it, I figured I'd reach out. I was also sort of wondering if the deer are still over there. I remember this time of year they take cover in those thick trees. I thought it would be neat to see."

"Oh, there are definitely deer," she says with a nod. "I saw a coyote once too. It'll be interesting to see if they stick around after they start all the construction."

I grow quiet as I take the exit leading out of town. The road is clear, but the patches of ground are snow-banked. After a moment, she looks at me. "So how was your morning? Pretty busy, I'm guessing with the team and all."

Before I over think it, I say, "You know, I'm going to offer Noah a spot on the team."

The air shifts into something heavy, like a bomb was detonated. Her smile fades enough as she barely whispers, "I didn't know that. Does he know?"

"I'll be honest," I continue with my eyes glued to the road, "Noah's one of the fastest guys who tried out, but he's a little too raw. I wasn't all that impressed with him at first, but you, you were...persistent."

Out of my peripheral vision, I catch her frozen expression.

"But—" I'm smiling bigger now as I add, "yesterday at the diner, I saw how he carries himself. He has the work ethic to step it up, and the right attitude, but he'll have to come in at one-thousand-percent."

She stares out the window and her voice appears timid when she says, "So, why are you telling me this?"

"No real reason. Maybe I was hoping it would bring a smile to your face." I shrug as I tug on the wheel, turning into a bend on the road. "I'll call him after I drop you off."

She turns back toward me, a playful smile on her face, "Well, in that case, take me home now."

That deserves a chuckle, and I laugh genuinely. "I could do that if you really want, but we're almost to the bridge." Then, more softly, I add, "And I'm enjoying your company."

It's her turn to grow quiet, and I focus on the road as it curves down toward the river, and I ease the SUV to a stop on the shoulder. Snow crunches under the tires, as if it's announcing our arrival. The old iron bridge stretches across the river like a dark skeleton against the sky, its reflection trembling in the running water below as if it's holding its breath until it reaches its final day.

We sit for a moment with the only sound being the humming engine. Ruth leans forward with her eyes fixed on the bridge. "It's crazy how for the longest time it just looked old. Now that I know it's being torn down, I think it's beautiful," she says softly.

"It's hard to imagine this river without it." My eyes trace the familiar lines of the rusted beams. "It's going to look empty."

"Right, it was part of a lot of memories." She points forward. "I remember floating on an inner tube underneath it. There's a bit of a drop right there, where we'd always wipe out."

I grin, as I can picture her doing that. "It sounds like you were a bit of a daredevil."

"Maybe, or maybe I didn't have the sense to know better back then."

We both laugh at that as we stare forward. For a second, it feels like I've stepped backward in time to a version of me who didn't have to think so hard about what came next. I glance over at her, and a glow lingers in her expression, making me wonder if she feels it too. I nod toward my door as I reach for the handle. "Shall we go for a walk?"

She raises an eyebrow. "You did see the snow, right? It's likely knee deep."

"It's not that bad. The sun's been shining. I bet it's hard," I counter, already pushing the door open. "Or are you scared?"

She scoffs and unbuckles her seat belt. "Never."

The cold hits the moment I step out, and I shove my hands in my pockets as the snow crunches under my boots. I round the SUV, and she joins me, wrapping her arms tight across her chest.

Trudging down the path toward the bridge, our breath clouds in the air as our boots leave prints in the untouched layer of snow. I take in the way the bridge rises in front of us. It's crazy how something man-made can seem to have a personality. It's weathered but proud. "I used to sit on that ledge by the first support beam," she says, not looking at me. "I would stare out, feeling like the world stopped spinning and nothing else existed."

I glance at the spot she's pointing at. I can picture her there with knees drawn up. "I remember," I say, "I used to stuff my pockets full of saltine crackers to throw into the water, thinking I was feeding the fish."

Her breath puffs out in a cloud as she chuckles. "I love saltine crackers, especially with peanut butter as a snack."

We creep right up to the edge and marvel at the bridge stretching out before us. She looks up at it with a soft smile. "It won't be the same when it's gone."

"No," I agree, my voice low. "But I'm glad we came. It feels like I owe it a goodbye."

Her eyes meet mine in the quiet pause. "I can't believe we never bumped into each other. You'd think we'd have seen each other at least once."

"Right." I shrug as I point back to the trail, and we both move along, going even closer to the bridge. I pull out my phone, turn on the camera, and hold it up, taking a few shots.

"Good idea," she says, following my lead, taking a few photos with her phone.

Turning my phone sideways, I play with the zoom, zeroing in so close I can see the dents in the steel. "Yeah," I speak more to myself, "it's probably time it goes. It's not in the best shape anymore." I zoom in even more and see a row of some of the largest icicles I've ever seen, hanging down like cave stalactites. "Wow, look at those." I move my phone closer to her, with it still zoomed in on the icicles.

"They look like crystals," she coos.

"I have an idea." I quickly stow my phone back into the coat pocket and wave her forward again, off the path.

"What are we doing?" Her voice pitches high with a mix of interest and delight. Her excitement only pushes me forward.

I nod toward the bridge with a small grin. "We're going to make one more memory here."

She tilts her head but doesn't press, and we carefully climb up to the bridge. I reach up and break off a long, narrow icicle from one of the beams. It snaps with a satisfying crack, and I hold it out like a prize.

She raises an eyebrow. "Are you planning to use that as a weapon?"

"Who, me?" I say with mock seriousness, offering it to her. "Nah, I thought it looked beautiful. Here, hold this up to the light. I want to try to get some photos of it reflecting."

The light hits just right, refracting through the ice, bending in soft shards of gold and blue. I take a few shots of it. When I examine the shot on my phone, I was right. It doesn't just catch the light. In the photo, the icicle looks like it's glowing from the inside—like it's alive.

"Hold it there," I say quietly, as I raise my phone back up and zoom in even more.

She stays still with the icicle in front of her, and the bridge rising behind her. I snap the photo, but when I lower the phone, I don't look at the screen right away. I look back at her and admire the way the light dances through the ice and reflects in her eyes. "Stunning," I murmur. *But I'm not referring to the ice anymore. She really has some of the most stunningly beautiful ice-blue eyes I've ever seen.*

She walks forward, peeking down at the phone, her arm brushing mine as she leans in. "Wow, that's a great shot. Now it's your turn to hold it, and I'll take a photo."

"Nah," I shake my head. "Nobody wants my big head in a photo."

"It's only fair." She pushes the icicle at me but I don't take it. Instead, I say, "I'll only pose with it if you agree to be in the photo too."

She rolls her eyes, but I catch the way her lips twitch before they pull into a wider smile. There's warmth behind it that hits me right in the chest.

"Chicken," she mutters under her breath, just loud enough for me to hear.

I raise a brow, playing along. "What was that?"

"Nothing," she says, the picture of innocence. Then, with a more dramatic sigh and a spark in her eyes, she adds louder, "Sure. If *that's* what it takes to get you in a photo."

I shake my head, smile, and hold up my phone again. She steps in closer without hesitation, the space between us narrowing until I can feel the soft press of her shoulder against mine. The wind has kicked up slightly, sending a few snowflakes dancing around us like a perfect picture backdrop. For a second, everything feels suspended.

We pose together. It feels natural, like we must show the world our favorite chunk of ice. It's exactly the kind of things I would have done when I was that kid who used to run around this riverbank. She's laughing when she playfully frowns and scolds, "Bill, you need to smile."

I look at the screen, but then glance sideways at her instead. Her cheeks are flushed from the cold. I grin, more for her than for me, because I don't care how the photo turns out. A niggling in my gut tells me this is a memory I want to keep. "Say, 'icicle' on two," she says as she moves the phone into a better position. "And smile!"

"How about icicle made *for* two?" I cut my gaze toward her right as she clicks, perfectly capturing the look of shock and wonder on her face.

She drops the phone and playfully looks at me, "What do you mean *for two*?"

"It sounds fun." I smirk and gesture toward the path again. "What do you think? Should we walk across the bridge one final time?"

Her gaze grows more thoughtful as I set the ice on the ground, and we step onto the wooden planks together. She squeals as the bridge creaks beneath us like it is counting every step. "I don't know if this is a good idea," she rushes out as she halts on her heel and nervously scans the worn planks.

"It's fine." Without thinking, I reach out. "Here, give me your hand."

She doesn't flinch as her fingers wrap around mine with quiet trust. We don't say anything as we step forward. The silence between us deepens as we slowly creep over the bridge.

After we've made it about halfway across, her free hand points forward, and she whispers, "Look at that."

I turn my head to see a small deer family standing near the other side of the bridge. Three of them. The biggest one, clearly a buck with large antlers, turns to watch us. Ruth and I halt.

Neither of us dares to speak. She lowers into a crouch, and I follow instinctively. Our shoulders brush as we huddle together, trying not to disturb the fragile moment. Hip to hip, shoulder to shoulder, we hold our breath.

The deer don't run. They stand there, watching the bridge while we watch them. It almost feels like they came out to say goodbye to the bridge too.

After a few moments, the wind seems to switch directions right as the sun slips lower. "It's getting dark soon," she whispers. "I hate to scare them away, but I should get back."

I feel her turn toward me, and I meet her gaze. Those stunning ice-blue eyes are wide, lit by that fading sunlight. I didn't plan for a moment like this when I invited her up here. I certainly thought we'd share a laugh or two, but unexpectedly the air between us tightens. Our faces are so close to each other's, and her breath mingles with mine.

Tension builds slowly, curling around my ribs, making it hard to breathe in that steady, normal way. I don't even fight it, as my instincts take over. My gaze drops to her lips. They're slightly parted, the dark pink stands out against her wind-flushed skin. I swear, for a second, the world narrows to only that space between us. Just her mouth, her breath, the glint of sunlight catching in her lashes.

I could kiss her.

We are that close.

It would be so easy to lean in and wrap my mouth around hers. I certainly got away with doing that to other women, but as I raise my gaze back to her eyes, I find something in them.

It's a vulnerability.

An unmistakable hesitation. That's what I listen to when I turn my head away. If I ever do get the chance to kiss her, I don't want to see any hesitation. I've turned my head with enough time to see the deer darting off, gracefully disappearing back into the trees. I whisper, "There they go."

"Yep," she whispers. "Goodbye, deer family." She exhales slowly as she straightens up, brushing off her coat, and her smile straightens into something unreadable.

"Shall we go head back?" I stand beside her with a heart rate that's louder than it should be. Automatically, I shove my hands back in my coat pockets, and we start trudging back the way we came. We don't say anything, but the air between us is soft and dreamlike, filling my chest full of quiet encouragement. So much so that I take a risk. My heart's hammering, not from the cold or the walk or even the almost-kiss we didn't have, but from the sheer weight of what I'm about to do.

I hold my breath.

Slowly, I pull my hand out of my coat pocket, fingers stiff from the cold, and from the hundred what-ifs rushing through my mind. The air bites at my skin, but I barely feel it as I extend my hand toward her and open it in offering.

For a second, she doesn't notice.

She's focused on something ahead, and I don't want to interrupt. When her foot creaks on a rotten plank, she glances down and sees my hand, just waiting for a reaction.

There's a flicker in her expression, and I start to take my hand back, but she slips her hand into mine, again. This time, it feels less like she's holding it for safety, and more like she's gripping on to something inside of me.

Like she's saying a very quiet *yes*.

We don't look at each other.

We walk the rest of the way across the bridge and all the way back up the trail to my SUV. When we reach the passenger door, I open it for her and smile. She exhales, which I can't tell if it's in disappointment or relief.

Maybe both?

"We made it," I say as I stand back for her to climb into my car.

"We did," she says, adding, "It's stupid, but I'm a little sad, knowing this is the last memory I will have of this place."

I glance at her with the fading light touching the side of her face, and the weight of what she said settles in my chest. "It's not stupid," I say quietly. "I feel it too."

I wait for her to get in, and I shut her door for her and hustle back to my side, get in, and crank the engine.

She shifts in her seat, turning slightly toward me, her eyes cutting at me with a bit of an angled slant. There's a glint in her expression that twists something low in my chest. "I wasn't sure why you exactly asked me to come, but I'm glad you did. Thank you. This was a wonderful way to spend the evening. I didn't even realize I needed to say goodbye to a bridge. It was so oddly healing."

"I'm glad you came. It felt more special to make this trip with someone else who also had fond memories, and now we have a memory of the bridge together."

"Right." She lets out an airy laugh. "We will always have our icicle for two."

I laugh too, as I shift the SUV into reverse. The tires crunch softly over the snow as I back away from the bridge, carefully cranking the wheel to turn us around. The sun's dropped below the trees now, casting everything in a rich honeyed gold that makes winter feel warmer than it is.

My hands move through the motions of driving us back to the main road, but my mind is far from automatic. I hadn't planned for today to be a date. That wasn't the point. I told myself this was about the bridge. It was supposed to be a casual trip with a touch of nostalgia, as we both shared memories

But now.

Now my heart is thudding like it missed the memo.

There's a pulse at the base of my throat I can't seem to calm. My palm still tingles from the weight of her hand in mine. And even though I'm focusing on the road ahead, my thoughts are still back there to what I swear was an almost-kiss.

I sneak a glance at her out of the corner of my eye. She's relaxed in the seat beside me, and her lips are curved in that quiet smile again. Is she thinking about that moment too?

"Who would've thought that would happen," I say, almost to myself, as I ease us onto the main road. "But it's kind of the perfect way to remember the day and our..."

I trail off, the sentence breaking apart in my throat.

And our what?

Our new friendship?

I don't know how to explain it, so I stop talking before I say too much.

She doesn't press me to finish the sentence.

But she's still smiling.

And somehow, that tells me she understands.

After a beat she says, "Yeah, it was the perfect day. To be honest, I was nervous. I didn't know if you were concerned about the bridge or if this was a... date," she admits, letting out a soft, uncertain laugh. "Or like... some sort of hockey loyalty test."

The sound of her laugh lingers, and I can feel her gaze on the side of my face. I honestly forgot about hockey. That's strange because I never forget about hockey or all the work I have waiting for me. My fingers tighten slightly on the wheel. I want to look at her fully. Instead, my eyes sweep to her for the briefest second before I force them back to the road and risk a weighty question. "Did you want it to be a date?" My voice is lower than I would have liked.

She exhales slowly. Then takes another full breath, before saying, "I haven't dated in years. It's not part of my life." She pauses for a beat before adding, "But I'm so deeply flattered you didn't cringe at the mere suggestion that this might have been a date."

I chuckle softly, but there's a tightness behind it, like I'm trying to keep something in check. I don't know why her reaction is affecting me this way. I go on dates a lot, actually. Nothing has ever been serious, as I swore off anything serious after Lacy tore out my heart in high school. Ruth is stunning though, she's certainly not even my usual "type" of woman as she has a son. She also appears to have some emotional baggage, but who doesn't at this age? I lock my eyes on hers. My voice rasps when I ask, "So, is that a no or a yes?"

She blows out another breath and looks at me. "Maybe it's that I'm confused why you'd bother."

My heart picks up speed. "What's there to be confused about?" I say, my voice is rougher now, more honest than I meant it to be. "You're gorgeous, you're funny, you know a lot about hockey, which is my favorite thing ever." The words hang between us, as if I also need to hear them. Saying them out loud makes something shift inside me. A quiet, undeniable thrum. Maybe I missed it earlier because at first glance she wasn't my type, but after spending the afternoon with her, I can see many things we have in common, including chemistry I didn't expect but can't deny.

"Look, I don't want to mess things up for Noah," she speaks gently. "As flattered as I am, I'm not looking to date someone who has a say in his future. And I'm definitely not looking to *help* him get places."

"That's fair," I say, my voice lower. "For what it's worth, I didn't think about Noah once since we talked about him earlier. This wasn't about him or my team."

She is quiet again before echoing her last statement, "I just don't want to interfere with what Noah has going on."

"That's what you *don't* want." I pull on the wheel again, taking a curve in the road, but use the slow down to sneak a fast glance in her direction. "What do you *want*?"

"No one's ever asked me that." Her voice is barely above a whisper.

My jaw is tight as I keep my gaze forward, making sure the road is clear because I glance at her again. This time slower, because I don't want to miss her reaction. "I'm asking you now."

The glow from the dashboard light paints her features in muted amber, enough that I notice the way her lashes flicker. Eventually she parts her lips. A word might've started to form, but she holds everything in.

I tighten my grip on the steering wheel, understanding exactly what she doesn't say...

Ten

Ruth

When I return home, Noah's standing in front of the kitchen sink on his phone. I take a deep breath as his gaze slams to me, and he eagerly points to the phone and mouths, "It's Bill Baker."

Flutters of nerves erupt from the very depths of my soul. My purse slides off my shoulder and drops to the floor with a thud, but I stand frozen.

Noah's stone-cold silent.

I watch his face like a radar.

He starts pacing in slow circles. After what feels like an eternity, his hand presses over his mouth, where he holds it there as if he's in shock. Then he exhales and flicks his gaze toward me while saying to the phone, "Thank you for the offer. It would be an honor to play for Granite Ice." His speech accelerates, words tumbling into each other. A sure sign he's bursting with adrenaline in the same way I am. A grin that might explode the roof off fills his face as he says a few more things, and then ends the call.

With his phone dangling from his fingers, he turns to me and whoops, "I made it!"

I open my arms as he practically leaps, grabbing me in a bear hug, lifting me off the ground and hollering, "I'm in the AHL!"

I've thought about this moment a lot over the years.

The exact moment his dreams come true.

I never pictured myself laughing, but I am now. Giggles of glee flow out of me, and tears well in my eyes. He sets me down, and I reach up and hold his face. It's the face of a full-grown man, but I enter a weird time warp in my head where I remember perfectly how his little face would fit in my palms. My pulse rises through my temples. "Congratulations. You earned it."

Noah's chin trembles, and it breaks me. He's never been a crier, even when he was little. "No, Mom, be honest. We did this together."

The fact he would take his moment to shine in pride and acknowledge my sacrifices cracks my heart wide open, unleashing the welled-up tears. "I'm really proud of you." I swipe at my damp cheek with the back of my hand and laugh again.

"Training camp isn't until fall, but I'm seriously going to start training first thing in the morning." His words come out with conviction, like he's saying an oath. I believe him.

"You're going to do great." I reach out, running my hands over the sides of his cheeks again. I can't stop looking at him.

He straightens up and says half-sheepishly, "Sorry to leave you, but I've got to call my friends."

"Of course." I nod, an ache budding in my chest as he hurries toward his phone for privacy. I get it. He needs to tell everyone, but I'm so honored I got to be the first person he told. I call after him, "Let's celebrate tonight. We should go to Red Barn for dinner."

"Sounds good," he calls back, but his phone is already pressed to his ear as he disappears into his room.

With him gone, I retrieve my purse from the floor and hang the strap on the coatrack next to the door, right as my phone chimes inside. I pull it out with hesitation and read the message:

Bill: Thank you for such a lovely afternoon.

A swell of happiness rises in my chest, despite my struggle to hold it back. Every second of our time at the bridge felt magical. Maybe it was the nostalgia of my childhood, but my gut tells me it's something more. I don't know how, but we have a chemistry I never expected. Yet, there's a niggling in the back of my head telling me to avoid Bill, especially now since Noah playing for Granite Ice is official. I certainly don't want to get hurt, or screw anything up for my son.

I stare at the message, my heart feeling both swollen and hollow. I can't just ignore him, but I won't lead him on. This needs to end now. I type out a reply and press send before I have a chance to change my mind.

It was wonderful to have a last memory of the bridge. Noah just got off the phone with you, and he's very honored by the opportunity, as am I. I'm looking forward to an amazing hockey season.

Hopefully, he gets the subtle hint that I don't plan to see him outside of hockey. Today was a one-time thing because of the bridge.

My usual breakfast rush has finally thinned, leaving all my booths covered in dirty dishes and sticky syrup. Like clockwork, I work through them to reset everything. I'm wiping off the last bench when the bell chimes over the door.

Casually looking over, my heart gives a flip.

It's Bill Baker.

"Good morning!" I'm a tad too eager as I straighten my apron and go on, "Are you here for the pancakes again? I had a feeling you'd be hooked."

He smiles back an easy grin. "Pancakes sound great, if it's not too much trouble."

I gesture toward the stool where he sat the other times he was here. "Of course not. Please, have a seat."

He straddles the stool and slips off his winter coat in one smooth motion. I stand back, farther than I normally would while taking an order, and ask, "Would you like coffee while you wait?"

"Sure, thank you."

I retrieve my notepad and scribble a ticket for Margie: big stack of pancakes. Then I slide the slip through the window. Since my morning rush has cleared out, it's quieter than usual, and I engage in small talk while I pour his coffee and slide it across the counter. "How's your morning going?"

My heart pounds in my chest while I scream at myself. *He's just a guest.* But then I remember the way we almost kissed, and my cheeks warm in recollection.

I don't do that with *guests*.

Something soft emits from his eyes as he eases into the conversation. "It's been good." He reaches into his jacket pocket. "Actually, I did something, and I came because I have a gift for you."

Completely shocked, I blink. "You didn't need to bring anything—" But before I can finish, he produces a framed photo, about the size of a Polaroid, and places it on the counter in front of him.

I barely need to look to know what it is. It's a photo of our bridge with perfect golden-hour light breaking through low clouds, illuminating the old beams to make them appear to be glowing. His voice softens. "I thought this might look nice on your photo wall. There's nothing more vintage in this town than that old bridge and, well, it's the last photo we'll ever get."

My breath catches as I stare at it.

Yes, it's a beautiful photo.

I'm happy to take it for my wall.

He's right, it belongs on my wall. So many residents will look at it lovingly, especially after the bridge is gone. Yet, it feels like it's so much more than a photo of a bridge. Something special happened between us on the bridge. Though we're content to dance around it, this is exactly the kind of gift that would melt any woman's heart.

My pulse hammers as I pick up the frame and trace the edges with my thumb, feeling so deeply the tenderness behind the gift. On the bottom of the photo, he's scribbled in black ink a caption: I'll *always remember our icicle for two.* Out of my peripheral I can tell he watches me with a softness that catches me off guard. I force the next words out with an even tone, "Thank you. This means more than I can say."

The pressure is on to say something to keep the moment light, but *that almost kiss* pulses sharply in my chest. Is this a way for him to nod to that moment? I can't help but think the photo has a bit of double intention. Of course, I'll remember that moment forever, especially when I look at this photo. I set the photo back on the counter. "You're right. It belongs on my wall where all the residents can remember it."

"Order up," Margie's voice blares from behind me, and I startle, warmth heating my cheeks. I turn and grab Bill's stack. Grateful to have something else to do, I slide it in front of him and return my best professional smile. "Enjoy."

I sense a bit of hesitation as his gaze drops to the pancakes and then back to me. "Oh, I will. Thank you."

Nodding, I head toward the farthest booth and commence my rewashing the tabletop, feeling it best to be busy away from him so he can eat, and my heart rate can normalize. I've never had some instant chemistry with someone like I feel with him. It would be wonderful if I was looking for romance, but I'm clearly not.

Eleven

Bill

(Three Months Later)

I step through the arena doors, which are wide open, welcoming the entire community of Mapleton to unveil the new facility just a week ahead of training camp. There were a couple of weeks when I didn't think we'd open in time, but it's amazing the sense of urgency people have when you throw enough money at it.

Today, we're hosting a carnival with booths, games, and concession stands. My Granite Ice players mingle with the crowd for their first official team meet and greet. It's festive, and I love it. It's exactly how I envisioned the place when I thought of our ribbon-cutting event. Mapleton has received this great team with open arms.

I stand near the plexiglass with my hands on my hips, trying to act calm and not like I'm holding back a tidal wave of emotions. I cannot wait to see this place packed for our first home game. The arena smells so clean and new. Now my team is home, and as I glance around, I still can't believe it's all real.

"Bill Baker?" a female voice cuts in from my right.

I blink and turn. It's a reporter with a *Mapleton Times* logo on her jacket. She's holding a camera and smiles politely enough. "Would you mind if I get a team photo for the front page?"

"We'd be honored." I turn back to my guys and call out in a loud voice, "All right, players! The paper needs a press shot. Everyone line up in front of the glass." They move, most of them being silly at first, striking a few dramatic poses. A couple try to look tough but ultimately ruin it by grinning too large. Taking my spot on the far end, I cross my arms and stare forward with my best game face on.

Because of course, I'm going to look tough.

The woman centers herself and takes a few shots, but that's not the only person with a camera aimed at us. A line forms of locals all holding their phones up, taking the same shot. I certainly didn't expect this, but it feels good. Pride fills my chest, and I stand still as people file through, all grabbing their photos.

And then I see someone I know.

Ruth steps forward, lifting an old-school, clunky camera with a strap around her neck and a giant flash attached to the top. It instantly reminds me of her love for vintage things, and I smile as her gaze meets mine for a split second before she raises the camera in front of her face. The click of her camera is audible, and my breath hitches.

Months have passed since I last saw her. Yet seeing her now feels like a punch to the heart. We went on that one casual date. It shouldn't seem like much, but our conversation was easy, and that spark was darn-near electric.

I never stopped thinking about her, but when I went to visit her at the diner the next day, she was polite and then almost ignored me. I got a vibe that she was giving me the brush-off. Taking the hint, I kept myself distracted in the bustle of getting my team started.

Now she is here, and I can't take my eyes off her.

The photos are done, and the team breaks formation as everyone heads into their own clusters. I step forward, closing the gap between Ruth and me until I'm a mere arm's length away. While she adjusts something on her camera, I clear my throat. "It's great seeing you here."

She slowly lowers the camera then offers me a toothy smile. "I couldn't miss the big opening. It's the most exciting thing to happen to Mapleton in years."

And just like that, the noise of the arena fades, and it's just the two of us.

It's crazy how that happens.

The chemistry between us is pulsing. Knowing I only have a few moments with her before I'll get pulled off in another direction, I rush to say something, "You look... great."

Then I cringe.

That was too direct.

I mean, she does look great in her blue jeans and sweater with her long hair down her back, but that compliment definitely feels blunt and burns hot on my cheeks.

"Thank you." She tilts her head away from me, like she's not quite accepting the compliment. "I'm excited for the season. They did an incredible job on the arena."

"They did." I stuff my hands in my pockets, rocking back on my heels. "I couldn't be happier."

She smiles at me, and I'm about to say something when Noah walks up beside her. He's got a foil-wrapped cheeseburger in one hand, and he pulls another foil-wrapped burger out of his Granite Ice jacket pocket. "Here, Mom. I know you prefer to snack but," he says, handing the burger to her like it's a prize, "I got this for free."

She raises an eyebrow but takes it. "You *got* it for free?"

"Yup," he says, clearly proud of himself. "The concession stand worker said since I was on the team, it was free for me."

I bite back a laugh as Noah digs into his jacket pocket yet again and removes *another* foil-wrapped burger. This one is flattened, and he holds it out to me. "You want one, Bill?"

I glance down at the burger, then at his jacket pocket, then back at him and wag my head. "I appreciate the offer, but I'm not sure how I feel about pocket burgers."

Ruth chuckles as she nudges Noah with her elbow. "I don't know how many more you have in there but maybe don't take any more. Save them for someone else."

He shrugs while still holding the extra one. "It's not a big deal. They're free."

Ruth looks at me and then back at Noah. "They're not free. I'm sure Bill is paying for them."

I hold up both of my hands in a stop motion. "Hey, you know what? You keep eating them, and I'll just deduct them from your salary."

Noah blinks, and Ruth laughs again. The sound of her sweet laughter sticks with me, like something I heard in a dream. I catch her eyes for a moment before she grins at her burger while shaking her head.

"Excuse me, Bill." A man wearing a concession T-shirt taps me on the shoulder. "I'm sorry to interrupt you, but I can't seem to find Cleo. I don't have a key to the pantry, but we are completely out of hamburger buns, and I need to get in there to get more. Would you have a key?"

"Out of buns? You don't say." I shoot a suspicious glare toward Noah, who raises his hands in innocent surrender, before I add, "I know we ordered enough buns to feed the entire town and half of the next one over." Pulling my giant key ring out of my pocket, I fidget until I find one that I have no idea what it belongs to and figure I can start with that one. Then I look over at Ruth. "Excuse me. Bun crisis."

"Of course," she says quickly with a tight smile.

"I'll bring them over to the stand." I tap the concession guy on the forearm as I step aside. I can't help but give Ruth one more glance and freeze as I catch a flicker in her eye.

Is that flicker for me?

Or maybe it's just the bright lights reflecting...

If only I had at least a few more minutes with her. Shaking my head, I stride toward the hallway, muttering, "This wouldn't have happened if people weren't taking eight extra hamburgers for their pockets. Now I must leave Ruth during my one chance to talk to her in months. Who knows when the next time will arise that I'll be able to run into her. Maybe it's no use."

Twelve

Ruth

The moment Bill fades down the hallway, muttering about burger buns, I allow my shoulders to drop.

Phew.

Not that I'm upset, but I was distracted. Like my body is too aware when he's near, and I have the hardest time relaxing. He kept looking at me like he was about to bring up something more personal. I don't need Noah to overhear anything.

I can't risk it.

Everything has been going so well for Noah. He has been managing his anxiety disorder, thanks to some new meds. I hate to be the cause of a flare-up if he starts to worry about all the things that didn't happen between me and his boss.

Yep, it's best I stay away from Bill Baker.

Coach Carlon claps loudly, aiming his attention toward the players. "Guys, take your places at the signing tables, so this can be somewhat orderly."

"That's my cue, Mom," Noah says. "This might take a while too, because the line is huge."

"Enjoy every minute of it." It's hard for my smile not to grow as he takes his seat at the table. Everyone from small children to elderly women line up to get my son's autograph. I stand back, snap a few photos, and then glance around.

Noah was right.

By the size of this line, signing will take hours. There's no need for me to stand over his shoulder supervising him. I side-step from the line, pondering the best way to get out of this huge arena. I'm not exactly fleeing, just strategically taking a breather outside the room. This way, when Bill returns from his bun emergency, he won't find me standing here and try to strike up a conversation.

I move toward the front entrance, but a wave of people swarms in from the lobby. Everyone is loud and laughing. It's shoulder-to-shoulder people with no way to move in the opposite direction. I pivot fast, as the only way I'm getting out of here is through the back exit. My gaze lands on a side door I never noticed before. Clearly marked with an Exit sign above it, but the door also says, *Employees Only.*

I pause and study it. From the location, my guess is it loops out to the parking lot. I cut my gaze to the back exit, which is clear across the packed arena. It could take me another ten minutes to force my way out of here. Bill will likely return by then. My gaze cuts back to the side entrance that's wide open, as if it's waiting for me.

If I'm fast, no one will even know I took that door.

That's the plan.

Just slip in and slip out the back door, and I head forward. *The crowd has other ideas!*

Someone elbows me hard in the ribs as I stagger on. The swelling crowd is more reason to take a breather outside. Before I talk myself out of it, I pass through the side door and cut into the dim hallway.

There's nothing out of the ordinary.

It's a long hallway with closed office doors on both sides. Halfway down the hall, light emits from one door that's cracked open. With the chemical tang of cleaner hanging in the air, I assume it's more than likely a janitor's closet. I slow as I approach, eyes darting toward the narrow gap.

Then I hear it.

Bill's unmistakable baritone booms from somewhere, echoing all around me, *"Why would you put the buns way up on that shelf?"*

I'm cooked!

I whip around, my eyes darting to find somewhere to hide. *He must be right behind me! This could be bad.* I don't think! I just duck inside the open door and smack straight into a warm, solid chest. "Oof!"

My hand flies forward, pressing myself off whoever this is, and packs of buns go flying in every direction.

I'm terrified to look!

My heart says I already know who it is when I cringe and make eye contact with Bill! "Oh no, I'm so sorry!" I say, stumbling backward. "I didn't know you were—"

"In an employee area," Bill says, one brow arched, trying not to laugh as a pack of sesame buns lands by his shoe.

I immediately crouch, reach for the plastic-wrapped package, and restack them on the nearby shelf, where the others are. With my heart hammering in my throat, I accidentally blubber out, "I was trying to avoid you. I mean—not *you* specifically. Just, you know all the people who came rushing in from the lobby. I was feeling claustrophobic and couldn't get out the front door. This looked like a short cut."

He chuckles low under his breath. "Yeah, I can't believe how many people are here. It's like the whole town showed up."

I stretch to grab the last bag I made him drop. My elbow bumps the edge of the door, just enough that it floats back, and I hear a soft *click*.

I freeze.

"Was that click—" I clearly am overstressed, as it shouldn't be a big deal. I find myself lunging for the door and tugging at the knob to check. To my horror, the knob doesn't even turn! My palms break out in a sweat, making it even harder to turn the doorknob, but I don't quit as I jiggle it and wiggle it in all directions.

"Oh, it must be stuck." Bill moves in, and I take a giant step away from him as he wraps his hand around the knob, giving it a firm rattle. "Well, that's interesting. It's self-locking." He pats his jacket pocket, retrieving a set of keys triumphantly, but pauses when he can't find a keyhole on this side of the knob. "So, it appears the door only locks from the *outside*. It's weird because there's no release on this side." He inspects the knob, testing it, but looks at me with a frown. "Okay, no, this is worse. Something's jammed. The latch must be faulty."

He pulls out his phone and dials, not saying anything. The only sound is the dull roar of the crowd in the arena filtering through the door. After a beat, he lowers his phone. "I'm trying to call Cleo, our building manager, but he's likely not even hearing his phone with all the noise."

"I can call Noah." Yanking my phone out of my pocket, I quickly tap out a call, but it goes straight to voicemail. "Well, maybe he can't hear it either, but I can text."

Hey, I got stuck in a closet that locks from the outside. It's down the hallway marked Employees Only. Come get me. I'm with Bill. Don't ask.

My cheeks warm as I stow my phone back in my purse and smile politely at Bill. "Noah should be here right away. Hopefully." I look around, seeing the stacks of pantry items. Everything from cups to ketchup to huge bags of chips, and it inspires me to crack a joke. "At least we shouldn't go hungry. We have all kinds of snacks."

"Right." He chuckles as his gaze floats over the shelves. "What kind do you like?"

"Oh, I like all kinds of snacks. It's actually my thing. I don't discriminate."

He reaches above his head and slides out a box of individual-sized chip bags, and opens it, grabs a bag of pretzels for himself, and holds the box open toward me. "Which kind is your favorite?"

"That's easy," I say, unable to resist a distraction and pluck out a bag, stating my selection, "Sour cream and onion." We open our bags and take noisy bites as we stand, staring at the door like it might spontaneously pop open any second. I shift my weight awkwardly as he clears his throat. "Well," he says, flashing a kind smile, "if I had to be locked in a closet with someone..."

I'm smiling a little when I reply, "I agree, there could be worse situations."

"Like who?" His smile turns crooked. "Who would be the last person on earth you'd want to be locked in a closet with?"

"Well, truthfully, not many people." I rub the bridge of my nose as I ponder how personal I want to get. Bill has this way of getting me to open up. He did it on our non-date. Now that I'm aware of that superpower, I resist it. "So, if we are going for real-life people, my great aunt Nellie, who wears way too much perfume. If we are making hypotheticals, I'd say Ross from that TV show *Friends*."

"How do you have anything against Ross?" Bill raises his brows, mocking shock. "He carried that show, especially the last two seasons."

"I don't have anything against him, but he's one of those book smart guys who has all the smart facts, but zero life skills. Like he can tell you all about the history of the door locks, and all about the evolution of technology, but he'd crashout if he had to stand here for any real length of time."

"Clearly, the panic was for comedy, but if that's your pick, then fair enough." Bill pushes out his lower lip into a thinking position. "I'll be honest, that's not what I was expecting. I'd have thought you'd say an ex or something."

"An ex?" my voice squeaks, as all a sudden we are in un-
charted waters. "No, I, uh, don't have many of those," I
say a little too quickly. "I haven't dated since I was married
to Noah's dad." There's a pause, just long enough for the
curiosity to settle in the air. "He passed away," I add softly.
"Asthma attack. It was just a normal Tuesday workday. He
was running late because he stayed behind to help me get
Noah ready for a doctor's checkup. Noah was just little and
a handfull. There was never enough time in the morning." I
offer a small, awkward shrug, like that somehow makes this
conversation less personal. "He never went anywhere without
his inhaler or his phone. Except that one time...because he was
running behind."

His expression shifts instantly as his jaw drops in surprise,
then something softer. "Wow. I had no idea," he says, his voice
low. "That must've been devastating. Especially with Noah
being so young." He goes quiet, which frankly I like that he
doesn't try to say anything to comfort me. That's the worst.
I hate when people pity me, or even more awkwardly make
a weird joke to cheer me up. He just stands there, and after
a pause says, "For what it's worth, you did an amazing job
raising him."

My eyes are burning. I need out of this topic, but since
I'm literally locked into a conversation with Bill, I revert the
attention back to him. "So, it's your turn. Who is your last

person to be locked in a closet with? Do you have an ex you can't stand?"

"I've got one of those." He nods for the fast breath before his brow lowers, and his eyes darken. "But ah, no, I'd be fine chatting with her. My last person would be a guy who once was my best friend. We played hockey together all through our childhood, and we both got recruited to the NHL. For a long time, we were inseparable. I trusted him with everything, including my girlfriend. I got sick on prom night, and I couldn't fathom being the reason she missed her senior prom. I trusted Blake with everything in me, and I begged him to sub for me, which ended up being a mistake when he stole her from me."

I blink, surprised he said it so plainly. "Wow. That's bold of him. And incredibly dumb of her. I bet she regrets that." I mean it to be lighthearted to cheer him up, but it's also true. The dude is a billionaire. I think it's every woman's dream to marry someone who can wipe all her financial struggles away. He doesn't say anything, so I add a little softer, "That must've really hurt. Losing two people like that." I tilt my head, offering a small smile. "Also, if it helps at all, I'm sure she's kicking herself now when she sees all your success, especially since you've been in the news so much with this team. She has to regret it every day."

"I've long since forgotten about her. It's his betrayal that haunts me, because Blake and I had been friends our whole lives. It felt like my whole life was a lie. I guess he taught me a hard lesson about trusting people. You never know who people really are."

"That's sad but true. It's hard to trust people." I nod with empathy.

"I guess learning those lessons is part of life." He finishes his snack and crushes the bag, stuffing it in his pocket before clearing his throat. "I've thought about you a lot though."

My breath hitches in the back of my throat, and I immediately jerk my gaze to the floor, desperate for somewhere to look that isn't his face.

Don't do this.

Don't look at him.

What am I supposed to say?

"Uh," I get out, but he speaks over the top of me.

"Did I do something wrong?" he asks gently.

I flinch and regretfully look at him, hoping he sees how I don't want to talk about it. "No."

He waits with wide eyes. It honestly breaks my heart a little, because he appears to think there's something wrong with him.

That was never the case!

"You were perfect," I say quietly. "Our non-date was perfect. You, bringing me that framed photo of the bridge to my diner was perfect. Everything was perfect."

I blink, but he doesn't give me a chance to avert his gaze as he is locked in. So, I swallow and drop the last part, "I just— I didn't want to mess up Noah's thing with the team. It feels a little too close there. Like a conflict of interest, and he's worked so hard to get where he is."

Bill shakes his head. "There is nothing you can do that would mess up Noah's spot on the team. He's a great hockey player. I'm happy to have him on the team, but that's honestly so separate from *this*."

Knowing a line when I hear one, I bite my lip. Sure, he says that now. What happens when I do the wrong thing or say the wrong thing, and things go south?

"You're a very good woman," he says. "I can tell by Noah, but not just that. I had an amazing time hanging out with you. We got along well and seemed to have a lot in common. I would really like another chance to get to know you." He doesn't smile this time as he holds a serious expression.

Boy, this little closet feels a whole lot smaller now!

It was small before, but it's like the walls are closing in as I try to find somewhere to fix my gaze. He takes a slow step closer, eyes searching mine.

Surprising myself, I don't look away. There's this crazy magnetism that locks our eyes together. My heart's pounding like it's trying to claw its way out of my chest.

This is stupid.

This is dangerous.

This isn't me, to get all swoony eyed for a guy with a cheap line.

And then he leans closer, peering at me with so much intensity my skin burns.

I can't talk.

I mean, what would I really say in reply to that anyway? *Uh, okay, Bill. That sounds neat.* Nope.

I've never been one who is good at this stuff, and I stare back at him as this invisible force takes over, pulling us closer. I can't explain what is happening. I'm pretty sure we're going to kiss this time. It's all over his face, and his eyelids begin to waver, lowering as he leans closer. I gently part my lips and...

BANG!

The door swings open with a violent push, and light floods in like a spotlight right before Noah bursts in, one leg in the hallway and one leg in the closet with wide, horrified eyes.

"Noah!" I startle as my eyes dart from him to Bill. "What are you—"

Bill and I spring apart like guilty teenagers. My cheeks fire heat, and I step all the way back to the wall, thankful Noah opened the door now, and not three seconds later when Bill and I would have likely been lip-locked.

"You texted me to come get you," he says. "How on earth did you two get locked in here together?"

Bill chuckles under his breath. I can practically feel the smug radiating off him. "I came in here to get buns." Bill turns to me. "Your mom got a little claustrophobic and was trying to find an alternate exit to get away from the crowd. She took a wrong turn in here because the door was open, but then she was surprised to see someone in here. At that point, she bumped the door closed, and it locked."

"That's messed up." Noah opens the door wider, motioning to it while looking at Bill. "And I'm pretty sure I broke it when I kicked it in, but I panicked thinking you'd die in there."

Bill chuckles again, not even giving the lock a second look. "Don't worry about it. It was likely already faulty."

Noah waves me forward. "Come on out, Mom. The crowd is thinning a little. I can help you find the exit."

"You don't have to—"

"I want to," he says, as he cuts a glance toward Bill. "I'll get back to the team in just one second."

Bill nods and waits for Noah and me to walk out first. Once we are down the hall a little, I glance over at him, my heart already swelling with pride. "So how did it feel to sign all those autographs?"

His grin is instant, and he spikes a hand through his hair. "Honestly? Weird, but awesome. Like, I kept thinking someone was going to point at me and say, 'Don't get his autograph. He's not that special.'"

We chuckle together, and I say, "No, that's not happening. I have a feeling this is only the start of it. You're sort of a big deal now."

We reach the end of the hallway, where there's an exit door right where I had predicted. Noah opens the push-bar door, holding it with one hand, and he teases, "Do I have to help you find your car before you accidentally get into a stranger's minivan?"

"Oh please," I scoff, laughing. "I'll be fine. This isn't my first parking lot. Besides, it's not the minivans I like. It's the white vans that offer free candy and snacks."

"Not funny." He shoots me a look as he continues to hold the door. I step through it but turn back, as I soften my facial expression. "Thanks for rescuing me."

"Anytime."

"I'll see you at home later?"

"Yeah. I think we have to stay late, but eventually, I'll get there."

My gaze lingers on him as the streetlights outside catch the gleam in his bright eyes. It's like all the happiness of his youth and his entire future ahead of him spiral together. I will never know where the time went. My heart feels like it's in a constant state of confusion. Many days I yearn for the little boy he used to be, but yet I'm so proud of the man he's growing into. I don't doubt for a second my brain is snapping a photo of this moment and storing it away for a later time when I yearn to return to this memory. "I'm proud of you," I say gently.

"Thanks, Mom." I wasn't going to hug him in public, but it's like he can sense I need it, because he reaches out, drawing me into a side hug. Taking the rare opportunity for public affection, I give him a good squeeze. Then I step back, wave, and turn toward the parking lot. I pretend not to notice him watching me as I stride all the way to my car.

My heart thuds like a rock in my chest. Not in the exciting way I'd expect for a day like today when Noah has so much success. Although, yes, it is surreal to see my little boy towering over me, charming fans, being a whole grown adult.

When I slip into my car alone, my mind stops thinking about Noah growing up and shifts to the way my gut flutters when I think of what just almost happened in that closet.

Did I imagine that?

I shake my head, half laughing, and I start my car and steer out of the parking lot.

If I know Bill, he's going to try to contact me.

If I'm honest, I sort of want him to.

Okay, not sort of.

I want to see him again.

Now what do I do? Nonchalantly text Noah and say, "Hey, dinner's almost done, by the way, I like your boss."

Yeah. No. That text is not going to happen.

This crush needs to stop!

Thirteen

Bill

The last fan waves as he heads out the arena doors. I return his smile, then watch as he disappears in the parking lot. The second the door shuts behind him, I exhale and lean back against the wall, letting the silence seep in.

It's been a long day.

But a good one.

No, it's a great day.

One of those days where dreams come true. It all went so fast, I almost feel like I missed half of it. I turn away from the exit and walk back toward Victory Hall, gathering up the stray flyers and a couple of empty water bottles that fell out of the overflowing recycling bin. This morning when we started this event, everything felt surreal.

Maybe like I was dreaming?

Now, the place feels *mine*.

Footsteps patter behind me. I turn and find Cleo carrying his overstuffed key ring on his way to the front door, likely to lock up. "Hey," I call to him. "I was actually looking for you earlier."

He raises a brow. "Oh, yeah?"

"The food storage closet has a lock that isn't working. I got stuck inside and had to call for help. One of the guys busted it open. You will need to check it out."

"Boy, I'm sorry I missed your call." He nods curtly. "Today was crazy with nonstop spills and things to take care of, but I'll look at the door first thing tomorrow."

"Appreciate it." I nod and watch as he locks the front door, as I expected. Turning back to me, he throws his hand up and waves before heading out. "Night, Bill."

"Night." And just like that, I'm alone in the dead silence. My heart hammers with something that's not quite adrenaline. I don't know what these emotions exactly are, but I'm not ready to leave this place. The day was so chaotic, I didn't have time to slow down and take it all in. Needing one more moment, I make my way down the corridor and step into the arena. Only the emergency lights are on, casting a dim bluish glow over the ice. Although it's a brand-new venue, I've already memorized enough so I don't need full lights to see.

I close my eyes, and it's all there: the stands filled with fans wearing blue and orange, the rumble of the bleachers after a game-winning goal, my team celebrating.

This is what I always dreamed of.

And now it's real.

I step farther inside until I'm right next to the boards, and I rest my palm against the cool plexiglass. *My dreams came true.*

But then the memory punches through like a slap to the face.

I'm twenty-three again.

Back when I was lightning on ice.

Playing in the NHL.

And there's Blake Anton.

No, excuse me while I properly introduce him into this memory: Blake Loser Anton, my ex-friend who stole my girlfriend and got drafted to my rival team.

Lacy was in the crowd that night. Maybe that made me on edge?

Maybe he made me on edge?

He came at me with his elbow high. All I remember is thinking I could get around him, but I was thrown up against the plexiglass, right as his elbow cracked me under the chin.

My head snapped back.

I went down.

Concussion.

My doctor said I couldn't risk another one, as that was my third. Just like that, my career was over.

The final score: Blake took my girl and my career.

For a long time, I stayed bitter, but then I came up with a new way to win—start my own team. Now, I scan the arena, and my heart fills with more than I would have ever dreamed about. I may have lost my career in the NHL, but this entire *team* is mine.

This dream is alive.

Even though I'm all alone, I can't help but smirk. "You didn't win, Blake," I say softly. "You did me a favor, because you pushed me to be even better. Every day I worked unceasing hours to become rich. I started buying little junky houses, fixing them up with my own labor, and flipping them to get down payments on bigger investments. One lucky deal led to another. Now I'm so rich, I have an empire, and I own a whole AHL team..."

A chuckle from the bottom of my gut erupts. It feels good to win. Surveying the empty arena, my heart swells. Then oddly, I find myself glancing to my side.

Then my other side.

It's not lost on me that I've done this all by myself. That's a point of pride for me. But as I stand here achieving my dreams, I can't help but feel like it would be nice to share it with someone. I've always been too focused on getting here to slow down for any relationship, or even friendships.

Sure, I have friends, but they are the sort of friends you use for social climbing and business. I never really let anyone fully into my life.

I couldn't trust anyone after what Blake did to me.

But now that I'm here, it feels like I might have missed something.

Just like that, a thought sparks.

I pull out my phone.

There might *be* someone I can text.

I open my phone and start typing as a new feeling seeps in.

Me: Hey, Ruth, I was thinking about you and wanted to make sure you weren't suffering from post-closet trauma. I stare at the screen. It's only been a couple of hours since I saw her. Maybe this makes me look desperate, but I'm hoping it comes off as more considerate.

I'm being a gentleman.

This has nothing to do with the way I keep seeing her smile every time I zone out. My heart slams against my rib cage when a text comes back.

Ruth: I'm fine. Thank you for checking.

Oof. That's a short reply if I ever saw one, and it feels a bit like a brush-off. The thing is though, that's almost her pattern. She takes a while to warm up, and my gut tells me to give it one more chance. **Me: I'm glad to hear it. I'm impressed by how well you handled the emergency. I think if you hadn't been there, I might have pounded down the door with impatience.**

Holding my breath, I stare at the three dots and wait for a reply. It takes a minute, and my nerves build in my gut so much I start to pace in a small circle. I let out a breath as soon as the text appears on my screen.

Ruth: Well, I would have yelled for help had you not been there too. It wasn't that scary since we had each other to talk to. It also helped there were tons of snacks, and I didn't have to worry about starvation.

I'm smiling as I construct another text and send it off right away.

Me: Right, the snacks were quite useful. If you must be locked in anywhere, I'd pick a pantry any day.

She doesn't respond right away, and I stare at my phone for a good couple of minutes, waiting for the dots to appear, but nothing. I drop my phone to my side, and gaze around the darkened arena one more time, before turning on my heel and walking out. My heartbeat slows, not in relaxation, but more of a conservation sensation, where I put up a guard and hope to not get disappointed. It doesn't look like she's texting back.

I stride back to Victory Hall and make my way through the lobby. I'm not thinking about anything in particular, except maybe how nice it would be to have someone special to share this moment with, but I guess life is funny like that. You can't have all your dreams come true. I'm not one to complain. I make it through the exit and all the way to my SUV, where I start my engine. I'm about to pull out when my phone vibrates with another text. My heart slams in my throat.

Ruth: Yeah, it was a weird night but glad it's over. Thanks again for checking.

My smile drops as I lower my phone to my lap and reread it. It certainly sounds like she wants to be left alone. I get that.

It was a long day, and I'm sure she is tired, but I can't help but remember the way she looked at me in that closet.

That wasn't a leave-me-alone expression.

Those were *kiss-me-now* lips if I ever saw them.

I don't think she's playing hard to get either. I truly believe she thinks I'll judge Noah on her behavior, and that couldn't be farther from the truth. I'm not ready to drop it, and I grab my phone and fire off another text.

**Me: Yeah. It was a crazy night, but I'm glad it hap-
pened because I enjoyed our conversation. I was hoping
you'd let me take you out for a real snack sometime...sort
of to make up for it.** Her reply hits my phone almost instantly.

**Ruth: I'm flattered, but I can't go out with you. You're
my son's boss. I just can't risk it. He's worked too hard
for this. Sorry.**

Exhaling, I read her text and feel no surprise. She never gave
me the vibe that she dates much, but . . . I always enjoy a
challenge.

Me: That's fair.

I set my phone down on the passenger seat and pull out of
the parking lot, all the while thinking of things I could have
said to her. However, I conclude, it doesn't really matter what
I say, because she seems to have made up her mind about this
"no dating." That doesn't mean I'm giving up. I'm just going
to have to take a different approach. I get to the stop sign and
grab my phone again. **Me: Okay, we won't call it a date.**

Her reply is lightning fast.

Ruth: Right, because it won't happen.

I exhale again and type the first thing that comes to mind:

**Me: How about a human encounter with someone
who owes you an apology for getting you stuck in a
closet?**

I hold my breath for three blocks and my phone lights up.

Ruth: Wow, you seriously don't take no for an answer, do you? Promise not to say anything even remotely flirtatious, or the human encounter ends immediately.

My smile is so wide that my eyes practically squint.

Me: I might be following your lead, as you don't exactly take no when it's something you want. And of course I will promise. I will text you the details tomorrow.

Ruth: I'm also bringing my own car.

My grin continues to tug even wider.

That was a yes.

Not a big yes, but a yes.

One thing about me is, I'm good at taking small wins and helping them grow into bigger ones. I don't know where this is going. Everything in my gut is pulling me closer to her. I must find out why.

Fourteen

RUTH

I don't sleep. I mean, I shut my eyes, but my brain flashes those texts over and over like some sort of weird texting marathon I can't stop watching.

For the life of me, I can't fathom why Bill is pursuing me. The dude is a bit of a legend, and not just in Mapleton. He was a phenomenal hockey player back in his day. He could have any woman on his arm.

Now, I'm lying here at 5:12 a.m., mentally inventorying every outfit I own and debating whether it's weird to wear heels to a non-date. I mean, I'm certainly not dressing up for a snack, because that makes me look like I'm trying.

I'm not trying.

But I don't want to embarrass myself.

By 6:00, I give up and do the unthinkable.

Don't do it.

I eye my phone like it's burning a hole through my nightstand. Clearly, I'm not thinking straight in my overtired state of mind. I snatch the phone, my fingers typing away before I have the willpower to stop them.

I type his name: **Bill Baker**

And I hold my breath as I wait for Google to find me all the reasons I don't want to see Bill again. He must have a criminal record. Unpaid parking tickets? Anything to help convince me this is a terrible idea.

Google pulls up a hockey highlight reel.

Okay. That's assumed since he played professionally. Out of curiosity, I click on it, and I'm instantly transported into an alternate universe where I'm watching him bodycheck someone into the boards. *Wow!* Uh, I've seen that done before, but when he does it, it's a little... something.

Or maybe a *lot* of something.

It is silly to watch this footage, as it's almost twenty years old! I click out of it, returning to my search page where there's an article: **"Former NHL Star Turned Investor Acquires New Subdivision."**

What? A whole subdivision?

That can't be right. I keep reading.

Another article: **"Bill Baker Donates $1 Million to Children's Hospital."**

Okay, so charitable. That's totally fair. It's easy to be charitable when you're rich.

"Former NHL Star Bill Baker Performs Life-Saving CPR and Saves Child's Life at Public Beach."

WHAT?!

Now I slam my phone down on the bed next to me.

Who is this man?

There's no way someone can be rich, charitable, good-looking, athletic, and save children's lives. The only thing worse is if I find out he's also rescuing puppies. I better not read that anywhere!

Being nosey, I retrieve my phone and scroll in desperation for a red flag. Ex-girlfriend drama? Misdemeanor for punching a fan?

Not a chance.

Just more shining spotlights:

"Bill Baker Hosts Gala for Shelter Dogs and Senior Cats."

Okay, I didn't mean that about the dogs!

Sweat springs on my brow. I mean, every rich person gives money to support animals. I keep scrolling until I land on something that nearly jumps off the page:

"Bill Baker's Runway Debut."

Wait! Just. One. Minute.

What is this all about? The date is older, from about ten years ago. I stare at the link for a minute.

No.

Do. Not. Look.

No good can come from looking at a photo of Bill Baker modeling.

With a tiny squeal leaking from my lips, I quickly shut my eyes and dare.

Click!

I open one eye, and there he is! A full-color, high-resolution photo of a younger Bill Baker—shirtless, smirking, doing some kind of jawline thing while posing in designer jeans.

And I drop my phone.

It hits the floor with a loud *thwack*. I freeze like I've been caught committing a crime. I don't need Noah to wake up this early, thinking someone is breaking in.

Scrambling to pick it up, I murmur, "Oh, no-no-no-no," like if I wish hard enough, the image of him will disappear.

It doesn't.

Of course it doesn't.

Bill's still on my phone, looking entirely like not-date material. If anything, it appears to burn brighter on my phone, like someone cranked up the screen light.

I should click out of it. Instead, I slap the phone back to my bed face down, while vowing to never, ever, again google Bill Baker.

Now that I've wasted enough time doing that, I have the opening shift at the diner to get to. It's not going to run itself. Maybe a few cups of strong coffee will jolt me back into reality. The kind where I don't get fluttery over a guy who holds my son's future in the palms of his hands.

I throw on a clean uniform dress, pin up my hair, and head out before Noah even makes a peep. It's still half-dark when I unlock the diner and flip the welcome sign to OPEN. I have barely switched on all the lights when the front door jingles open.

And there he is! Bill Baker with a good-morning smile aimed right at me.

"Wow," I say, blinking my eyes into focus. I still haven't had time to make the first pot of coffee. "Coming on a little strong. Don't you think? Our non-date isn't until this afternoon."

He shrugs like he isn't waltzing into my workplace with ulterior motives gleaming out the corners of that smile. "What can I say? You were right about the pancakes."

I narrow my eyes. This is way too early for any sort of flirtation, and I had clearly warned him. "You can take a seat but remember, you promised no flirting."

He gives me an innocent look. "No, I promised no flirting on our *non-date*. You said nothing about the *pre*–non-date window."

I roll my eyes and grab a notepad, adding, "pancake stack" to the top. "Would you like a side of bacon and coffee with your pancakes?"

"You are reading my mind already." He leans forward, lowering his voice enough to make my pulse skip. "That's clearly fate."

I quickly turn toward the kitchen window, mostly so he can't see the flush rising over my neck. "Walking in pigs and cakes," I say, handing the ticket to Margie, who gives me a knowing look and raises an eyebrow.

If I was looking for a man, this would be the time where I would loiter near the counter and find all sorts of ways to make small talk. *That's the last thing I need to do!* I quickly turn the automatic coffeepot on, then busy myself wiping down already-clean tables on the opposite side of the place, while my eyes keep flicking out the window as I pray for customers, so I can busy myself with them.

It's not lost on how Bill has settled onto his stool like he now owns it. His hair is a tad longer than what is normally deemed clean cut, but he wears it parted on the side, in a classic old-money part. His eyes do that crinkle thing when he catches me watching him.

Doh!

Why am I watching him?

I shake my head and mutter under my breath, "Get it together, Ruth."

But my heart doesn't seem to care. It seems like it's already planning what I'm going to wear to our non-date. Before I can stop myself, I blurt out, "So, do you care to give me any hints about our non-date this afternoon, so I know what to wear?"

"There's going to be snacks." His voice is even, like he has the itinerary already memorized. "And activity."

"Activity?" I echo with raised eyebrows, as that sounds a tad suspicious. I never agreed to activities. The coffeepot gurgles, announcing it's done, and I hustle behind the counter, pour his cup, and slide it across the counter.

"Don't worry about it." He winks as he takes his cup by the handle and leans back. "I got it taken care of. You just bring yourself."

"Order up!" Margie saves me, and I turn on my heel and grab his plate, setting it in front of him.

"Enjoy." I smile politely as the door opens again, bringing in a new table of customers, and I'm able to step aside, leaving Bill to eat.

I wish I could say my mind was put to ease, but it races full throttle all afternoon.

I drive right up to the fence and park under a crabapple tree that's stubbornly holding on to a few brown leaves, like it's claiming them to prove we won't have a winter this year. Kind of like what I'm doing, clinging to the fact this isn't a date.

Because it's not a date.

It's two people sharing a snack.

Two people who may, or may not, be attracted to each other.

Definitely not a date.

After killing the engine, I sit with my fingers wrapped tightly around the steering wheel. I take a deep breath, trying to calm my heart flutters. Then I stuff my small wallet into my oversized coat pocket, swing open the door and step out.

The chilly air bites at my knees, and the regret of my decision to wear a dress sinks in. It's my favorite shade of pink to match my coat. Now that I'm here, I know without a doubt, it's completely wrong for a winter "non-date." He didn't forewarn me about the outdoor part. At least I had the foresight to wear tights. Still, as I tug the hem of the dress and glance around, I feel completely overdressed. Yet, underdressed at the same time, if that makes any sense.

Bill's sitting casually on a park bench, wearing jeans, a Granite Ice hoodie, and a crooked smile that does *things* to my nervous system. The second his eyes land on me, his grin widens, which sends my heart ramping up even more. "Wow," he says as he stands and strides toward me. "You look incredible. Pink's totally your color."

I blink, all the while I'm yelling internally at myself for how terrible this is going. He's not supposed to compliment the color. It's my favorite color, and he's not supposed to notice that. "Uh. Thanks."

"Are you ready for this extravagant snackfest?" He gestures toward the stretch of sidewalk lined with food trucks. "There's a food truck festival today. So, it's a very casual non-date activity, but hopefully you find something you enjoy snacking on." He holds his phone out in front of us, where he has a list opened to the food truck lineup, and he starts reading, "Okay, we've got: deep-fried mac and cheese balls, pizza-stuffed waffles, cheddar tots, PB&J quesadillas, candy corn cotton candy, giant corn dogs, walking tacos, fifty-two flavors of lemonade, and mini donuts."

"That's a lot of choices." I run my hand through my hair, tucking back a few strays that seem to want to play in the wind.

He shoots me his mischievous smile. "You don't think you can handle it?"

"Oh, no, I can totally handle it, but let's walk and see what looks good," I suggest, tugging my jacket closed, and I fall into step beside him.

Large crowds of people pack the sidewalks, and the scent of everything from sweet, spicy, and salty aromas swirl this way. We move slowly, shoulder to shoulder, and the tight coil of nerves in my stomach starts to loosen. Maybe it's the fresh air doing its thing, but the more steps we take, the easier my breath is.

A couple walks by, wrangling not one, not two, but an entire six-pack of standard golden retrievers in matching sweaters. One barks, and the others follow. "Boy, it looks like they have their hands full," I say low so they don't hear as they pass.

Chuckling, he says, "Right, I bet there's never a dull moment."

We pause and watch them parade down the walking path. One of the dogs lifts a leg on a bush, at which point we turn away to give him privacy. "I had a dog when I was little," I say, not sure where the memory came from but suddenly unable to stop it. "Her name was Shoo Shoo. She was such a flirt. She would always run after the mailman and the delivery guys, but only on the days the male carriers stopped. If it was a woman, she would just sneeze at them. For the males, she'd never bark, but just wagged her tail, waiting to be petted."

"She sounds sweet. I have one dog. He's nearly twenty, and I got him right after high school. His name is Puck"

I blink at him. "Of course that would be his name. What breed is he?"

"Bulldog."

I nod, as it fits his personality perfectly. "Has he been a good dog to take care of?

"For the most part. He does have a problem with stealing and hiding my things. I have to make sure everything is locked up, because it's also the most random stuff that I would never think he'd want. Of course, it's always when I need the item he's hidden, and I'm low on time. Sometimes it drives me to the near point of insanity, but I love him."

"That sounds exhausting."

"It can be, but it's the game he plays and loves."

We're both grinning now, and a comfortable silence settles between us for a beat, until he glances over at me. "Okay, I have a very important question, and you have to be honest."

I raise an eyebrow. "Who said I wasn't honest?"

"Oh, you absolutely are." He stops walking and stands in front of the waffle truck. "What's the weirdest food combo you actually like?"

I know exactly what to say, as I have a weird favorite food that spurred during my pregnancy with Noah eighteen years ago, and the cravings never left. However, it's more than a little weird. I'm not sure he's ready to hear this yet, so I pretend to think, stalling, and say, "You first."

"Fine." He straightens with too much confidence. "I love an ice-cold Coke with olives in it."

My mouth drops open. "What?"

"I know it's crazy, but once you get over the ick factor, you will find it's not much different than a beer with olives. That used to be my favorite drink, but I gave up drinking booze years ago and was looking for a substitute. This is what I landed on. You should try it sometime."

I gag dramatically and turn my shoulder to him, acting like he's suddenly contaminated, and I don't want to look at him. "I feel like you shouldn't tell people that."

"What? It has fizz and salt."

"All right, fine," I say, lifting my hands in surrender. "Mine is just as bad. When I was pregnant with Noah, I craved two foods and only two foods. I couldn't get enough of them, so I started mixing them together in a bowl."

He freezes. "This is going to be gross, isn't it?"

"Tuna with butterscotch pudding."

"That's"—he makes a sound halfway between a groan and a gag—"so disgusting?"

I shrug, not offended at all because I know. "I blamed the hormones for a long time, but really it's not much different than putting mayo on tuna, and how many people do that?"

He presses both palms to his face like he's in pain. "No, Ruth, it's a lot different than mayo."

"I stand by it," I say sweetly. "If I have to try your Coke olives, you can try my butterscotch tuna."

He peeks through his fingers, mock horrified. "You realize I'm totally judging you now."

I lean in a little, biting back a smile. "And I you, but you started it."

A spark gleams out of the center of his eyes, making me enjoy the conversation so much more. In a way, it feels like we've been friends for a long time. "What do you think?" I jerk my thumb over my shoulder to the waffle truck. "Should we start with the jalapeño waffle stick?"

"You would want to start with that?" He laughs but doesn't hesitate to get in front of the truck window, ordering us both a big waffle stick with raspberry dipping sauce. It's not something I'd normally eat, but it's a beautiful day. I'm up for the challenge.

He hands me my waffle stick, and I dip it in the sauce and then raise it to my chin as I try not to get the sticky jelly paste all over me. When my teeth sink into the first bite, I can't resist and I hum, "Mmm."

"That's good." He takes the words right out of my mouth, and he motions to the bench off the path. "Should we sit over there?"

I don't even reply because I'm too busy enjoying another bite. I simply walk forward and plop down on the bench. He takes a seat beside me and points to the jungle gym behind us. "Did you see that climbing thing over there?"

"Yeah?"

"I once got stuck on the very top of that thing. I kept climbing higher and higher, not taking the time to see how tall it was. When I reached the very top, I panicked and froze."

"How was that for you?" I stare at him over the top of my waffle stick, not slowing as I nibble off another bite.

"Terrifying, actually. My mom tried to coax me down, but I was completely stiff. She eventually called the fire department. You'd think the near mention of having to call for emergency help would have scared me enough to try to come down, but nope. They came with a small engine. For a moment, I thought I would get to ride in the bucket ladder, but they didn't need it. One of the men climbed up and carried me down under his arm. Of course, I cried." He grins, pleased as he adds, "And I got ice cream."

"Oh, you poor little boy," I say, giggling. "I bet your mom was relieved though. Little boys are so much work."

He shrugs his thick shoulders. "She probably was, but I think I was more relieved."

We both bite off the last of our waffles, neither of us in a hurry to let the moment go. We linger side by side on the bench like something else is supposed to happen, but we just don't know what yet. I'm not hungry enough for another snack, but I also don't want to go home yet.

He crumples his napkin and stands, stretching his hands over head and walks a few steps over to a trash bin, tossing his garbage away with an easy flick of his wrist. I do the same, making sure to brush the stray crumbs from my coat and straighten my skirt. That's when he holds out his hand.

Not for a high five like a good job on doing your part to not litter.

But an open palm of invitation.

"Skate with me," he says, voice steady, like he already knows I'll say no and has a solid plan to counter all my excuses.

I glance toward the small ice rink a few yards away, the edges lit up with string lights. It's actually the same ice rink where they held Granite Ice tryouts, and where I first saw him. The memory alone is enough to make my heart ramp up, but someone's playing old love songs through a portable speaker, and suddenly, I'm swooning.

Still, I shake my head. "You know, I haven't been on the ice much since Noah was little, when I taught him how. I'll likely get us both killed."

"You'll be fine. I promise to catch you if you fall," he says, not dropping his hand. "Come on."

I hesitate and turn to look back down the path to my car. I mean, we came for one snack. I held up my end of the deal. I could leave now and feel pretty okay about it. I shift my focus back to him waiting with his palm still open, gaze fixed on mine like I'm the only person here.

And for some reason, I give him my hand.

My fingers slide into his, and the moment we touch, something inside me stirs. We stride together to the icehouse, where we grab a couple of pairs of rental skates. My hands tremble as I lace them up. I'm not only terrified of skating, but of where this whole thing is going to take me with Bill, and not in a destination sort of way. I'm silent, allowing him to take my hand again as we step onto the ice, and we take slow, careful steps. I'm beyond awkward, trying to shuffle forward with straight knees, but he shifts his position, placing his closest hand around my lower back, and he holds my hand with his other hand, putting his side into a hip-to-hip lock that robs the breath from my chest.

Being in his arms is electric.

And terrifying.

It's terrifyingly electric.

Or electrically terrifying.

I'm not sure of the proper order of words, but I'm positive those are the correct words.

He skates forward, but he has some superpower where he doesn't actually have to watch where he skates because whenever I steal a fast side-eye, his gaze is on me. His hand presses firmly above my hip, just enough to remind me I'm not flying. Though now I feel like I am. Around us, the music plays, and we avoid a kid who whizzes around the rink, darting in and out of other skaters. Bill looks behind him, staring after the kid, and says, "He's got wheels, huh?"

"He does. Reminds me of Noah at that age. He just never had any fear," I say, as we finish our lap and start another one. A breathless laugh escapes me, and he smiles like he's proud of making it happen. I feel like a teenager again, wrapped in a crush that's quickly spiraling into something deeper.

His fingers tighten into mine, and my heart trips in my chest. We keep skating around the outside of the rink, locked in a rhythm that isn't perfect, but it's working. We skate until the song is over, and I leak out the last of my nerves in a giggle and grab the wall, ready to breathe. "Don't make me do that again."

He places one hand on the wall, leaning in right next to me, but leaves the hand that was on my hip in place. For a moment, I check it, as it seems a little odd to have to hold me up, when my hands are both firmly on the wall. Then I turn my gaze back to him.

Before I know what is happening, his hand tightens even more, drawing me to him, and he leans down until our lips are only separated by a breath. I pause a second, maybe two. Just enough to feel his warmth.

Have I lost my mind to behave like this?

And in public?

Someone is bound to recognize me.

I pull back quickly, turning my face, heart pounding, while my lips tingle with the kiss that didn't happen. He exhales slowly and covers his mouth with his hand like he's trying not to move too fast.

"Sorry." I smile, small and shaky. "I should probably get home."

He nods while a serious expression takes over his face. "I'm sorry if I crossed a line."

"It's fine." I don't look at him as I step over to the exit and continue to the icehouse to return my skates and get my shoes. The silence stretches. It's thick with tension and every time I sneak a look at him, he's giving me a heated gaze. My heart races, tangling up into a mess of want and confusion.

This was a bad idea.

Who really thinks a non-date is going to stay a non-date?

I'm screaming at myself for being such a fool, all while we walk to the parking lot, and I reach my car and fumble for my keys in my pocket.

He shifts beside me. "I don't want to leave it like this. I don't want things to be weird. I wasn't trying to do anything that makes you uncomfortable. I know we set boundaries about this not being a date "—he glances at the ground, shifting his weight from one foot to the other, and then raises his gaze back to mine—"but skating with you like that to that song just did something to me where I momentarily forgot, and it was my fault. I didn't mean to upset you."

"You didn't upset me." My words tumble out with a shaky breath as I can't believe I'm about to be honest. Before I lose my nerve, I go on, "I liked it. That was the problem. I liked skating with you and being here with you. I liked it all a little too much."

His brows soften as his gaze hovers over me, trailing from my eyes to my lips and back again. There's something unspoken in the way he looks at me. It's tender and intense, like he's fighting the urge to dive in again.

I don't say a word.

For a brief moment, I focus on my car as my brain seems to be sending out a last warning to me to get in and drive away before everything changes. I don't heed that warning. Instead, I turn back to him, and against my better judgment, I tilt my face up and stare into his eyes.

He leans in so slowly, my lips are practically burning by the time his breath brushes mine, warm, inviting, and I feel it all over. My heart ramps up. My stomach tightens. The distance between us shrinks to nothing. Suddenly I forget how to stand.

His eyes flick to mine one more time.

And for a moment, I can't breathe.

Because I don't want him to stop.

I want him to kiss me so badly, my lips part.

He dips a little closer. His nose brushes mine. The air between us thickens.

His lips barely graze mine for a whisper of a second that sets every nerve in my body on fire. I sway into him, drawn like gravity, but I catch myself in time and turn my head away while my breath catches in my throat. My whole face burns, and I don't dare meet his eyes. "Sorry," I murmur, though I'm not sure if I'm apologizing for pulling away or for wanting to kiss him.

He doesn't move, but his tone is a little hoarse. "You don't have to be."

I finally glance up, and the way he's looking at me is almost too much. "It sounds so bad, and like a cheesy line, but it really isn't you," I say, "It's just...you know, I can't do this, and I really should get home."

"I get it." He nods, releasing me gently. I put one hand on my door, but he beats me to the door handle as he reaches around me and opens it for me. I hop in, but he shifts his body in the space between my door and my seat, blocking me from closing the door. He stares at me intensely. "Can I call you?"

No!

I want to tell him to go before I do something reckless again. But the words stay on the tip of my tongue.

Not when he's looking at me like *that*.

He's got one hand propped against my car door, his body angled enough to cage me in, without actually touching me.

It's maddening how close he is, how aware I am of the heat permeating off his body.

His other hand rests casually in his pocket, but there's nothing casual about the rest of him. His shoulders are broad, likely from all the years of playing hockey. His mouth is slightly parted, like he wants to maybe say something but hasn't decided how to say it. Maybe he's thinking about kissing me again?

And don't get me started on his eyes!

They're locked on mine, and there's so much tension rising from my body my pulse races.

He has to know exactly what he's doing to me.

The curl of a smirk tugs at the corner of his mouth. It's not a cocky grin you'd expect from someone with his credentials. There's softness underneath it. Yet, the gleam in his eyes betrays him. He wants to kiss me more.

And maybe I do too?

He shifts, sloping a fraction closer, and my breath hitches. His scent, clean and fresh and something totally *him,* wraps around me like a shield I didn't ask for. I press my back into my seat, trying to create distance between us when there's nowhere to go.

Because he's not touching me, but I can't ignore him while he's this close. "Do you always look at people with that smirk?" I ask, trying to keep my voice even as my breath shortens.

"Not people. Only you." He arches a brow, languid and self-assured.

Oh.

I don't even know what to say. If he wasn't standing in my way, I should slam my door shut and just leave before this gets out of hand.

I don't.

Instead, my mouth parts.

Nothing comes out.

Just a breath.

He leans in slightly, voice low and smooth, his voice rough at the edges. "Tell me to leave."

"Leave." It comes out quickly, and we both chuckle.

As if to test me, he shifts his weight away from me, as if he's ready to leave. I don't say anything. I need him to leave. "It's just that we're in public. Someone could see us, and Noah. This is going to be weird for him."

His lips purse out, as he backs away a small step. "Got it. I'll walk away, but I'm going to call you later."

I open my mouth to tell him no, but my body betrays me. I don't get a word out. So, he shuts my door and stands back as he flashes his palm up to wave goodbye.

I crank the engine with urgency, yelling at myself for ever going on a non-date with Bill Baker.

Who knew a non-date would turn out to be the best date?

Fifteen

Bill

The warmth of the diner hits me first, calling me inside. It's hard to believe I've lived in this town for most of my life and never experienced this place before meeting Ruth. Now I'm fast becoming addicted to the sweet scent of maple syrup and their delicious pancakes, and well, to be honest, Ruth.

She's wearing a messy ponytail and a white apron over a pink dress. Pink is just her color, and it does something to me. She doesn't notice when I seat myself in my usual counter stool. I wait patiently, trying to ignore the pounding in my head. It's one of those migraines that has burrowed deep with slow throbs behind my left eye. The pain is nothing new, as I've suffered from migraines since my career-ending head concussion, but it never gets easier. Crazy, yet, after all of these years, I still never have a clue of when they will hit. I went to bed on cloud nine, high from our date, and woke up feeling like a truck hit me. I tug off my Granite Ice beanie and lean onto the counter for support as I breathe into the migraine.

Out of my peripheral, I see Ruth turn toward me, a flicker of surprise landing on her lips before she arches a playful brow at me. "You again?"

"Don't sound so disappointed." It's easy to smile, even though my face feels like cement with more pressure building by the minute.

"Are you here for food or to try to relentlessly flirt with me?" The angle of her smile tells me she's open to some banter, and my heart flutters hard.

Wagging my eyebrows, I say, "How about a big helping of both?"

She tries to mock being unimpressed but her lips twitch. She goes on, pretending to be professional, "So, Mr. Baker, pancakes, coffee, and bacon?"

"Unless you've got a cure for headaches."

Her eyes narrow. "Are you hungover?"

"Not a hangover. More like a twenty-year leftover." I try not to grumble as her smile is so sweet. "I had a concussion when I was playing in the NHL, and the aftershocks have been content to linger all these years."

With her brows dipping down in the middle, she leans one hand on the counter in front of me. "Wow, that's a long time to suffer from an injury."

Not wanting to be a downer, because I didn't come here for pity, I force a playful smirk. "Just enough to remind me I'm not invincible."

Her eyes pace around my face. "Hang on a second, I have something. I've nursed a few hockey injuries in my day." She disappears into the kitchen, reappearing a moment later with a small bag of crushed ice wrapped in a dish towel. "Here." She nudges it forward. "This might numb the pain long enough that you can eat."

"I don't need that," I say, pushing it back. "I'm tough, remember?"

"Right." Her lips curl into a beautiful, flirty smirk. "I forgot. I'm talking to a former NHL star. You are definitely tougher than a bag of ice."

A chuckle slips from my lips, but it's paired with instant regret as my head pulsates in protest.

I swear her eyes soften as she watches me, but the door jingles open, and her gaze is instantly averted as she rushes out, "Noah."

I turn more with my eyes than my body to the door. Sure enough, Noah's grinning, totally at ease as he first spots his mom, but his gaze quickly shifts to me. "Hey, Bill," he says, sliding onto the stool next to mine. "I didn't expect to see you here."

"Hey." I give Ruth a sideways look, but she's turned her back to me, filling my coffee cup. "I came for the pancakes," I say, right as Ruth places my coffee cup in front of me with a polite smile. "How was practice?"

"Good." He gives a solid nod.

"Did you have a good morning?" Ruth asks him, her voice even.

He shrugs, peering at me and then back to her. "Yeah, we had a lot of drills and a ton of skating. I'm starving. Can I have pancakes and a burger?"

She doesn't seem surprised as she pulls her pen out of her apron and writes on a ticket. "Oh, to have an eighteen-year-old metabolism again," she mutters under her breath before she slides the ticket through the cook's window. Instead of turning back to chat some more, she grabs a pitcher of ice water and walks around the room, refilling everyone's glasses.

And I understand.

Noah is her kid. Although I know him, it's an odd thing. Like, she's not ready for me to be included in sharing this part of her life with him.

Noah is her whole world, and I'm basically a side character of that world right now. A side character, who can't stop imagining more slow kisses with her... My heart ticks up as if competing with the pounding in my head. It's as if my heart is trying to tell me my path forward: The key to Ruth's trust isn't going to be the banter that works on other women. The key to her heart is through Noah.

Because he is her heart.

I turn slightly, resting one elbow on the counter and face Noah as much as I can, without splitting my headache open worse. He helps himself to a glass of water and scrolls his phone.

"So, Noah," I say, nudging him lightly with my elbow. "Who are you going for in tonight's game?"

He perks up instantly, aiming his sharp eyes on me. I notice immediately those eyes are mirror images of his mother's, and I barely hear him say, "Florida."

I wince dramatically. "I thought we were going to be friends."

A chuckle slides from his lips as he shifts in his chair, redirecting his attention back to me. "What is there to hate? They have a tough defense, and they're fast."

"True." I nod, getting a flashback. "I played against them back in my day, and they aren't easy to keep up with. You're fast too though. I actually think you could keep up with them."

"Thanks." He nods slowly, like he's letting my compliment sink in.

I steal a glance toward Ruth. She's wiping a clean counter with her back toward us, but she's not looking at the counter. She's looking straight ahead, giving away that she's more than likely listening.

My heart kicks hard, reassuring me this matters.

I turn back to Noah. "Hey, listen, I'm glad you're on the team. I want you to know if there's anything I can do to help you succeed, I'm here for you. I want this to be the best team."

Shrugging like he's trying to be humble, he says, "Well, if you're willing to give me advice, I'm all ears. What would you do if you were me?"

"That's a great question." I narrow my eyes before I decide even that hurts too much. What I wouldn't do for a pair of sunglasses right now. I just didn't think the pain would be this strong. I should have stayed home, but I couldn't stop thinking about Ruth, thus, here I am. Taking a deep breath, I give Noah the best advice I ever got from a coach. "So, a guy in your position needs to pass more than shoot. At least for right now. You are fast and get out in front of the team. Passing will get the guys to trust you, and you can work on your shots in the meantime. You will get there."

He blinks twice and slowly nods. "That makes a lot of sense."

Trying to fight the magnetism that keeps me looking for Ruth, it's no use. This time when I find her, she's returning from a booth of customers, and she's staring right at me, and my breath hitches in my throat.

The look she's giving me confirms I've found her love language.

Bingo.

Sixteen

Ruth

I slide two mismatched plates onto the counter, a red plate for Noah, and a blue plate for Bill. "Here you go," I aim for casualness and pray they don't see my hands shaking. "Enjoy."

Bill reaches for his silverware and looks directly at me. "Looks amazing."

My heart flutters as I get the double meaning. "Flattery gets you decaf," I reply flatly, and Bill snickers low in his throat. That smile. I hate how much I like that smirk.

Standing back against the counter, I wait for him to take his first bite. Instead of eating, he glances at Noah as he cuts his first pancake. "Did you notice all the road construction on Main Street? Seriously, what are they thinking about, doing that this time of year? It's going to be buried in snow soon."

Noah throws his head back and grumbles with annoyance. "They always do that. All summer long we're forced to deal with potholes. Then right when the snow flies, boom, they make an even bigger mess."

"It's unreal." Bill plops a bite into his mouth. "I used to attend all the city hall meetings, trying to talk some sense into the clowns. They won't take anyone's opinion. That's one of the reasons why I built our arena out of town. I can't handle the city's lack of leadership. If I had it my way, I'd be on an island."

I move to refill a coffee mug across the diner, pretending I'm not listening. But I'm listening. Oh so intensely while my heart thrums hard.

Noah goes on, "It seems like every other year Mom is fighting with it here too, and it's months of low business, because no one can get in the parking lot."

"You're right," Bill says simply. "They usually rip up this road. Sometimes it doesn't even need it. I think the city has contracts with their friends and get kickbacks. It's a yearly paycheck for them, living off the taxpayers, while wreaking havoc on the traffic."

Moving to a table in the back, I busy myself cleaning finger smears off the window, but thank goodness their voices carry. They've returned to a conversation about hockey, which sounds so natural it tugs at my lower gut. I head into the kitchen, fill a few more orders, and circle around to the front again.

"Wait, you actually like that band?" Noah's voice cuts in through chuckles.

"I know they're old," Bill replies. "But that's what was playing on the speaker when I was in the NHL, and I'm transported back instantly to my best days."

I catch myself smiling as I wipe down the back counter, even though I've wiped it at least ten times.

It's like watching two parts of my life collide in slow motion.

One I never expected to matter.

One I've protected with my whole heart.

They found a way to click together, and it terrifies me.

Since my late husband passed, I've never dated, and even if I were to date, I knew I'd always be the mom who would never let a guy get close to my kid. That's not the mom I am.

This is exactly the kind of moment I don't trust.

Bill's phone rings, and he excuses himself from talking to Noah as I head toward the register to ring up a regular's tab. From here, it's easier to hear exactly what Bill is saying, "Yeah, I know. I'm not in the office now. Can we hold off on the call for another hour? I'm having lunch with a friend."

I freeze with my fingers poised over the register keys.

Did he just call Noah a friend?

Not a player on his team.

I glance back in time to see Bill put his phone face down on the counter and return to their conversation without missing a beat. Noah's eating with his full focus on Bill.

He's in it.

And me?

My heart is pounding like I ran a marathon.

Because I'm watching my son, who I've protected from everyone, and this man who has every reason to walk out that door to tend to whatever business was trying to pull him away but chose to stay. They're laughing like they've known each other for years.

My hand finds the front of my chest, and I hold it there while I take a deep swallow. Man, I want to believe this is genuine. It's so scary to think about what opening my life, and Noah's life, would actually look like. We've been just the two of us forever.

I turn away, heading to the kitchen, but not because I don't care.

I care *too much*.

Seventeen

Ruth

Warmth generates from the freshly tumbled towels as I roll them like the spas do and stack them into piles on the couch. Noah's voice carries from the kitchen, where he joins in the chores, doing his best to sweep. He's been talking nonstop since I got home. Not that I mind. I love it, as it reminds me of how he used to be as a young boy. It's just not his typical self since he entered his teens, disappearing into his room with earbuds and his phone. I usually consider myself lucky to get a grunt.

"Did you hear Bill say that I was fast?"

I roll a hand towel and keep my voice light. "I did hear that, and you are fast. Are you ready for the first game? It's coming up."

"Yeah, I'm always ready for ice time, but did you know what?" He doesn't wait for me to answer. "Bill said I need to pass more than shoot. Then later he said I could be a little more vocal. I was thinking about that after lunch, you know? I think he's right. It sets you up to be seen as a leader if you can communicate well. He's so smart."

I blow out a heavy sigh. Bill is consuming Noah's mind. If I'm honest, he's sort of all I can think about too. It's overwhelming. At least I used to be able to come home, where Noah and I had our own little family that was safe from Bill. I pause with my hands still on the towel. "You talked about leadership?"

"Yeah." Noah takes a few steps out of the kitchen with his hand still wrapped around the broom handle. "He said real leaders aren't loud all the time, but they need to know when it's right to speak up."

I bite the inside of my cheek as I desperately dig for a matching sock, like that sock is going to save me.

Because my son bragging about Bill Was. Not. On. My. Bingo. Card.

Noah never had a male role model he connected with. That's why I nudged him into sports. I purposely sought out the best coaches, but they've never been the one-on-one a boy needs. The coaches cared, but they had rosters to manage. They didn't sit with him and give advice over pancakes. I clear my throat, wishing it was that easy to clear my anxieties. "So," I try to steer back away from Bill, "are you ready for practice tomorrow?"

"Almost. I might retape my stick tonight. Bill said it is good luck." He leans back, smiling like he's had the best day of his life. After a beat of silence, where I risk an easier breath, he adds, "It was fun though. You know, talking to Bill. He's not like what I expected for someone who played pro and also owns the team. I wasn't nervous to talk to him at all. He was like a friend."

I force a pinch-lipped smile while my insides twist.

This feels like things are falling into place without my permission.

Noah's still smiling when he turns around, heading back into the kitchen. I sit on the couch, folding the same dish towel three times before I realize I've already folded it. I set everything back in the basket and catch my phone lighting up from the coffee table.

Bill's name is glowing on the lock screen.

Thanks again for lunch. It was the highlight of my day seeing you and getting to talk to Noah.

Seriously?

I shouldn't reply.

But I want to reply.

But I shouldn't *want* to reply.

My fingers move before I can drop my phone.

He liked talking to you too. Thanks for being kind to him. *Send.*

I barely set the phone down before it lights up again.

Can I see you tonight?

My heart stutters. *Boy, he doesn't mess around.* I look at the clock. It's late. Too late to tell Noah I'm running an errand.

It's kind of late. I don't want to have to explain to Noah why I'm leaving the house after I already took all my makeup off. I never do that. He'll worry.

I set the phone down again and waltz into the kitchen, busying myself with wiping my counter. One thing about Bill entering my life, my counters have never been cleaner. I've wiped them all down again and am working on the front of the fridge when Noah's phone pings. He retrieves it from his pocket and says, "Hey, Mom, I'm heading to JD's for wings with the guys from the team."

I blink. "Wait, what? I fed you two meals at the diner. How are you even hungry?"

"I've been training." He moves toward the front door, slips on his shoes and jacket, but pauses to look back at me. "Besides, wings are just a snack. Nobody can get full on wings."

"Okay, try not to be out too late. You know I can't sleep well until I know you are home, and I have to be at the diner at five again."

"Sure thing. I'll be back by midnight. I have practice tomorrow too." He strides forward while typing on his phone and closing the door behind him.

Without pause, my eyes cut to my phone.

I pick it up and do something I would never have thought I'd ever do.

Me: Actually, Noah just left with friends. What do you want to do?

He answers in seconds.

Bill: How about wings at JD's? It's bucket night.

I shake my head, smiling despite myself.

Me: I like wings, but not JD's. That's where Noah's going. Actually, anywhere public might be a risk.

Bill: Okay. Not JD's or anyplace public. I could pick them up, and we can eat them at my place.

My stomach flips. I stare at the message as my breath catches. *I'm not going to his place! Is he insane?*

Me: That's way too private. I'm not ready for that.

His reply is quick:

Bill: Okay. Not my place. Somewhere public but not public, and private but not private. I have an idea, but it's a surprise. Meet me at the diner.

My thumb hovers. My heart races. Every part of me is screaming at me for doing this. Well, every part except my heart. Before I talk myself out of it, I manage a simple:

Me: Give me twenty minutes.

Eighteen

Bill

Flurries swirl through the night air, dotting the windshield with winter sparkles. I leave the engine running, lean back in the driver's seat, and watch the dark windows of the diner.

Ruth pulls up next to me and gets out of her car, pulling her pink coat tighter around herself, while her usual knit hat is tugged low over her ears. She sprints forward with her head down like she's trying to avoid winter.

The tops of her high cheekbones turn a little redder with each second they fight against the wind. I step out of the car, hustle around to her side, and open the door for her.

"Hey," she says as soon as she sees me. "Where are we going?

I smirk as I wait for her to slide into her seat. "What part of *surprise* don't you understand?"

A puff of laughter leaks out of her lips. "You're lucky I trust you."

"I am lucky." I whole heartedly agree and shut her door before running around to my side of the vehicle. I hop in and shift the car into drive. The sound of the tires crunching over the parking lot snow fills the silence before I sneak a sideways glance at her. "I feel like I'm seventeen again with all this sneaking around."

"Sorry." Her tone is soft. "I wish I could be more free-spirited about things. I don't know how Noah would feel if he knew I was with you. This feels like it's his business."

I glance at her, serious now. "Don't be sorry. I understand." She peers at me with lifted eyebrows, perhaps asking me to prove my understanding. "I mean it. I totally get it. You don't want to upset him, but honestly? I don't think he'd care. I think back to when I was his age, I had my own goals, but I absolutely wanted my loved ones to be happy too. He's not a little boy anymore. I'm sure he'll understand that you need a life."

She turns to the window, and I stop talking, as it seems like I might have said a little too much. I don't mean to insert myself into her business. It's clear she's thinking about her son, which is a wonderful thing, but she needs to know that, sometimes, she can think about herself too, especially now that Noah's out of high school.

A song starts on the radio ticking into an 80's beat that I recognize immediately as a Tina Turner classic.

Ruth's lips twitch. "I remember this song," she begins with words seeped in laughter. "I wore that wig to a party once."

"You think that's funny?" I grin as I decide whether or not to tell the truth, but it's so easy to be myself around her, and I dare. "Here's my confession. I had her poster in my room."

Her jaw drops into a fake gasp as she whispers, "No."

"My mom joked it was the biggest hair on the wall. It was in between a poster of Casey Jones from Teenage Mutant Ninja Turtles and my first broken stick that I mounted like it was a trophy."

She covers her mouth, laughing. "I hate to say it, but you're ruining your image. You had me fooled. I thought you had class."

"Nah, not ruining it at all." I chuckle while keeping my eyes on the road. "I'm very versatile. Plus, that was what, the late 80's or early 90's me, when I was like ten or maybe twelve?

What else was I supposed to be obsessed with then?" I offer a relaxed shrug and drive.

Because right now, this is enough. I don't need to talk. Every few seconds I catch her lips twitch like she's struggling not to sing along. She obviously knows all the lyrics, but she's pretending to be cool, and it's adorable.

When I turn onto the old frontage road that leads around the railroad tracks, she glances at me while lifting a suspicious eyebrow. "Okay, you totally lost me. Where are we going?"

"Remember we talked about how this is a surprise?"

"Right, and did I tell you I don't really like surprises?" She chuckles before she adds, "I would be fine if you ruined it for me."

I take the final turn, making sure to drive in an arc that allows my headlights to sweep across the faded sign for *Mapleton Drive-In*. The field is dark and covered with a few inches of frozen snow, as it's long since closed for good. I park under one of the old speaker boxes that's partially capped with snow.

Her gaze flicks to the large screen, then back at me. "I'm so confused. This place is condemned. What are we doing here? Also"—she holds up her index finger as if she needs to make an important point— "if that screen turns on, I'll need you to race out of here because it's clearly haunted."

I can't help but laugh as I reach behind the seat and pull up a to-go bag with the JD's wings logo on the front. "We wanted some place private but not, and some place public, but not. This is the best I got."

She lets out a surprised laugh. "Oh, wow, you really did deliver on that, didn't you?"

"I'm a man of my word."

"You're also incredibly sneaky."

"I'm versatile, remember?"

She shakes her head, and her smile grows even wider as she gazes out the window. "So, are you sure we should be here? It's clearly not open."

Cajun seasoning aroma escapes the bag as soon as I open it. I take my time neatly pulling out a stack of napkins for her and one for me, and then hand her a box, which she takes with wide eyes. "Only the finest, late-night-illegal-chicken operation in town."

She snorts, popping the lid on the box. "Seriously, so you just admitted we shouldn't be here. Like we can get in trouble."

"It's fine." Part of me wants to let the excitement of trespassing linger as it has a way of making this feel a little more exciting, but I'm not one to be cruel. "I actually own this plot of land. When they closed it down, the city was going to demolish everything and turn it into a new development for lots. I got all sentimental and decided to buy it, so they wouldn't wreck it."

"Seriously?" Two little lines wrinkle on the top of her nose. I'm not sure if I ever noticed them before, but they are cute. "Are you planning to reopen it?"

"Serious as a heart attack." I pop my lid open and grab my first wing, but I hold it for a second as I finish my thought. "I never planned to open it. I just didn't want to see something so full of the town's history get leveled into condos. I guess that's what happens when you get old. You start caring about things that have history." I let out a chuckle seeped with nostalgia.

"That isn't about getting old. I am the same way. I love vintage things. They seem to be built with more heart. Thus, why I have a whole wall in my diner devoted to all the things."

"You know, I don't recall any photos of this place on your wall..."

Her head tips to the side, as if she's thinking. "I don't think there are any. I have never been out here."

"We can't have that. Your wall should have all of Mapleton's most important history. We need to grab one some time."

"That's a great idea." She wipes her fingers with a napkin and leans back in the seat. "You know, when Noah was younger, we'd eat in the car a lot, especially during tournaments. It was sometimes the only way to get a meal between games. It's crazy how fast that time flew by. Now it feels like it's been forever since we did that. There's just something different about the way a car meal hits."

"I eat in my car all the time."

She looks at me, half-skeptical.

"Why does that surprise you?" I pause and wipe my fingers.

"It seems like your life would be a little too fancy for that."

"Ha." I throw my head back and toss up an exaggeratedly loud laugh. "My life is far from fancy. In fact, my life maybe was a lot like yours and Noah's, growing up on hockey. I used to sit in parking lots with my buddies after practice. We'd dig in the seats for enough change to get fries and then listen to the radio for hours, as we all wondered why we never had girlfriends yet."

That earns a loud laugh. "I have a hard time believing that."

"It's true." I tip my head to the side and add, "Well, when I think about it, the lack of dates might have been due to our obsession with hockey. There wasn't much time for anything else, especially when my goal was always to make it to the NHL."

"So, you didn't date at all in high school?"

"Oh, I did..." My words drop off as I weigh the words that come next. I used to hate talking about Lacey, but today it barely gives me a pause as I say, "Remember, I shared with you how I had my first love, and she broke my heart when she ran off with my best friend. After that, I was over being serious about a girl, but I had fun being not serious with lots of girls."

"That's too bad, but in a way, that's sort of my story too. I had my one, and then I didn't…Though, I didn't go out with lots of men after that ended."

We eat in comfortable silence, passing the wings back and forth between plastic containers, dipping sauces balanced on the dashboard. Outside, the snow keeps falling.

"Did you ever try those burritos at the truck stop by my diner?" she asks when she's finished the last of her wings. Her eyes narrow as if she's about to disclose a horror story.

"Yeah." I lean forward, grinning. "One time when we were on a bus trip home from a game. It was amazing going down. I'd like to think I blocked it out, but I clearly remember being in the bathroom for two days."

She groans as she shakes her head in comradery. "It was the best of times eating it, and the worst of times removing it."

I laugh so hard I grab my chest to steady my breath. "I have to admit, I never thought you'd be one to make a joke like that."

"Oh, please. There is no joke about it."

I can't help but stare at her. I'd like to think it's me who makes her cheeks flush like that, but it's likely the wing sauce. She's undone the buttons on her coat, making her appear relaxed and at ease being with me.

She's beautiful like this.

And my chest tightens.

Not with nerves.

It's that sensation I get whenever she's around. As happy as I was, I didn't realize I was missing this, whatever you call it—doing everyday things with someone. Suddenly, it doesn't feel so ordinary.

I finish the last of my wings and take a moment to gather all the trash back into the bag and then return the bag to the back seat. She leans back in the seat, her breath fogging the window. "So," she says, her voice quieter now. "Why do you think you're still in Mapleton?"

I hike my finger over my shoulder, pointing to the empty sack of wings we just devoured. "Did you not just eat those wings?"

She gives me a *very-funny-but-give-me-the-truth* look. "You and all your businesses have clearly outgrown this little town."

I smile, but the question lingers in the back of my throat. I can answer most things honestly, but this one is hard. "I've certainly left for years and traveled. I guess when I decided to start my own AHL team, nowhere else made sense. I wanted a team filled with guys who had heart, and it led me back here...to home."

There's a soft beat of silence, where she studies me like she's trying to truly understand what I just said.

Then I risk it. "Can I ask you something?"

She hesitates before saying, "Depends what it is."

"It should be no secret by now that I like you." I'm sur-prised by how easy it is for me to say this. "What do I have to do to be able to take you out in public?"

"I'm so sorry about this." She chuckles softly. "I know Noah isn't a little boy anymore, but I don't want to risk anything unless I know it's more than a casual thing."

My chest tightens. It definitely is a sign of strength for her to choose not to date casually. I'm guessing it got lonely at times. In an odd way, our paths mirror each other's. I dated casually, and that's all I did. I haven't had a single relationship that lasted more than a few dinners with plenty of beautiful women. Never once did I want anything beyond that.

Until now.

Something about doing ordinary things with Ruth makes everything better. That thought doesn't give me anxiety in the way it would with all the other women I've known. It actually puts me at ease. Maybe it's because she's treated me so differently, not wanting anyone to see that she's friends with me. All the other women always wanted elaborate dinners out so people could see us together. It felt like they wanted my money and status more than me. This feels so different. I need her to know that. Ruth's watching me with an expression I'd diagnose as guarded.

I clear my throat. "Do you know something?" I don't wait for her to reply. "You're the only woman who's treated me like a person and not a dollar sign in a very long time, but more than that, I like who I am when I'm with you. It's hard to explain, but it just feels right."

For a second, she doesn't say anything, so I take a chance, as I'm ready to show her how much I mean these words.

I lean toward her.

Right as I get close enough to feel her breath on my face, she turns her head, just a little, but it breaks the moment.

My stomach wraps into a giant knot in the pit of my gut, and I stop, letting my breath fall between us and whisper, "What is it about me that is making you so guarded?"

"I'm sorry," she whispers. "It's not you. I know that's the most cliché thing to ever say, but it's so true. You've been wonderful. So funny, kind, and thoughtful. It's just that it's been Noah and me for so long. Some of the years have been so painful as I struggled to heal, and I can't do it again. I'm terrified to let someone in because I can't ever go through a heartbreak again. It's the reason they call it a heartbreak, because it broke me."

I open my mouth to argue that I understand how she feels but it's worth it, but she keeps going. "And honestly, I'm still a little flabbergasted about why you want me. Don't get me wrong, I'm deeply flattered, but you could have any—"

"Stop," I say, as I dare to place my hand on her arm. "Don't do that. Don't sell yourself short. You're smart. You're strong. You're hilarious. You're incredibly resourceful when you're locked in a snack closet. Maybe a little too tenacious when you want something, but it adds to the fun. You love things, even when they are old and worn out, long after everyone else has given up on them. I could go on."

She stares at me with wide eyes.

"I get that it's hard to trust, but I think this time it's going to be worth it. For the record, I'm not dating anyone else," I say. "And I'm not going to disappear the second this gets inconvenient."

She blinks again, a little glassy-eyed now. "What do you want from me?"

I hesitate, shifting in my seat. "I want what you feel comfortable giving, but if I'm being honest, I want to give this a real shot. Like one where we tell people we are dating. Sure, it's fun sneaking around, but I want to give you more than that."

Her gaze avoids my face as she seems to look past me out the side window. "I don't know," she admits after a while.

"Okay." I nod, thinking of something I can do to get her to see I'm not playing a game. "Then how about this?" I take a breath as I come up with a plan on the spot. "Let's take a weekend trip together. Just the two of us."

Her head whips around so fast it's almost comical. "What?"

"I'm serious. I understand you don't want to risk the rumors and all, but let's go somewhere where no one knows us, so we can go on proper dates. Then if you still aren't sure about me, I won't ask to take you in public again."

"That's crazy."

"It's not."

She opens her mouth, probably to tell me I've lost it, but I steal her hand from her lap, holding it steady. "Look, I'm not trying to pressure you. Everything will be on your terms and at your comfort level. Clearly, we'll have separate rooms. You don't owe me anything. I just want to spend time with you, where you aren't so nervous about, you know...all the things."

She stares at me, mouth open slightly.

"We can do whatever you want. We can shop at cheesy boutiques or play board games for all I care. Shoot, I'll even let you win. I just want some time."

"You're insane."

"Possibly." A half-grin tugs at my lips. "But I'm hoping it's very charming."

She shakes her head, but the corner of her mouth betrays her, twitching like she's fighting a smile. "This is insane."

"Yep. You already said that much, and I already agreed."

I stare into her eyes, finding a flicker of something in them. Unsure of what she's thinking, I stay quiet, and eventually she spits out, "Okay."

I triple blink as I wait for my brain to catch up to my racing heartbeat. "Yeah?"

I've seen her casual nod so many times. This time it feels weighted. "Just one weekend."

The tight knot in my stomach unravels in one glorious, spinning moment. "You won't regret it," I assure, my voice coming out with a bit of rasp as I try to be cool and hide how emotional I am.

Her eyes glint with a layer of something I can only describe as hope. Swallowing hard, I vow to do everything in my power to earn her trust. "I hope not." She glances around the car, like she's about to get out, before she looks back over at me. "I hate to cut this short, but I should be getting home, especially now that I have to plan to be gone this weekend."

"For sure. We can take a photo another day. Maybe in the spring when the weather is nicer." I was so distracted, I never noticed, the heat from the vents filled the car so full of hot air, the windows had fogged up all the way. I crack a window and turn down the heat as I shift the vehicle into reverse, and slowly back out as the windows clear.

She's quiet as I drive out of the snow-crusted field. After I pull onto the main road that heads back to town, I peer over at her. "Are you okay?"

I wait as her lips purse out. And then, softly, she says, "It's been a long time since I did anything for me, and I'm looking forward to a vacation. I think it sounds amazing."

"Good." As we move closer to town, the radio cuts in with a loud cackle, and an 80's beat fills the car. We both groan in unison. She has a knee-jerk reaction and turns the radio knob to off, as she blurts out, "I can't listen to that."

A chuckle fills my throat, and I can't hold it back. It's hard to explain the feeling inside of me. It's easy to be with her. I tap the steering wheel as I steal another look at her, while keeping my eyes on the road. "I really like your coat." The words are out before I realize I let them go.

Her nose scrunches as she gives me a side-eye. "My coat?"

"Yeah. It's pink and I like it on you."

Her cheeks flush, but she doesn't look away. "Thank you. Pink is my favorite color."

"That makes sense because you wear it a lot."

I turn onto a familiar road, and she's still peering at me when she says, "You're not what I expected."

My heart slams against my chest as it feels like she's about to compliment me, but after she turned her head on that kiss, I'm feeling awfully vulnerable. "Good or bad?"

"I'm not entirely sure yet, but I have a feeling I'm getting closer to deciding."

I grin. That feels like a win for now. I turn into the diner parking lot, where the streetlights cast a warm glow over us. The snow's picked up, falling faster now, but she doesn't move when I pull up next to her car.

"I'll text you about the weekend?" I offer.

She nods. Her eyebrows bunch together, into what I now know is her thinking expression. "Okay."

"Pack comfortable shoes," I say, going for levity. "And your favorite board game."

She rolls her eyes but then quickly latches her gaze back to mine. "There's no way we're going to play board games."

"That sounds like you're afraid of losing."

She laughs as her hand slides to rest on the door handle, but she doesn't open it. Instead, she says, "Thank you for the wings, and for... you know, not pushing."

"I'm not in a rush."

A glisten in her eyes tells me she's processing that. I keep one hand on the wheel, squeezing it tightly when she opens the door, and the frigid air rushes into the vehicle. If there's one thing I've learned tonight, it's she's a strong woman. I'm not pushing anything. I can watch for signs she may want help, but she's clearly fine. She surprises me by leaning back in and dropping a kiss on my cheek. It's light, quick, and warm, but in the most innocent way, it steals my breath away. "Goodnight," she whispers as she backs out of the car and shuts her own door.

I wait, making sure her car starts and watch as she drives out of the parking lot. "I'm not in a rush." I let out a breath, repeating the last thing I said to her, "Because I'm not going anywhere."

Nineteen

Ruth

It's Friday afternoon, and I've worked the entire day. The bell over the diner door jingles, and I glance up from behind the counter where I'm filling a tray of waters for a huge table. Noah struts in, his hair still damp from his after-practice shower. Silently, he plops into a booth and shrugs off his jacket. Forgoing a traditional hello, he says, "Mom, I'm starving."

"You always are." I grab an extra cup, filling it with water and pass it to him as I take the tray to the table in the back. Giving them time to peruse the menu, I return to Noah's booth.

"Practice was hard," he groans, defending his hunger.

I take a guess at his appetite. "Meatloaf today?"

"That sounds perfect." His gaze slides to his phone as I scribble his order on a ticket. Nerve bubbles fizzle in my stomach, but I figure now is as good of a time as any to break the news. I press my palms to the edge of the table, lean in a bit and speak in a hushed tone, "Just an FYI, I'm going out of town for the weekend, and I'll be leaving here after my shift."

He continues to stare at his phone before his gaze slides up to meet mine. "Wait. What?"

"It's a little getaway." I wave dismissively, trying to downplay how nervous I am. "I'll be back Sunday."

His brow hikes, and he stares at me like I'm a stranger. "Since when do you have plans?"

I laugh, because it's a valid observation. "I have gone out of town before."

"Yeah, for restaurant supply runs, food shows, or maybe a funeral." His brows dip low and his tone drops. "This isn't like a secret surgery you aren't telling me about?"

"No, it's not a surgery. It's for fun." I shrug, acting like it's no big deal. "I decided that I need a little break, and you're finally old enough to fend for yourself."

He narrows his eyes into slits. "Who are you going with?"

My stomach somersaults. "Uh..." I glance around the place and sigh with relief as it's slow tonight. Nobody needs me right this second. I hate to lie to him, but I'm confident if this weekend goes the way I think it will, I can tell him everything very shortly. I sink on to the bench across from him as I murmur, "Just me."

With his phone clenched in his hand, he doesn't take his eyes off me as his gaze bounces around my face like he's inspecting it for clues. After a beat, he says, "Good for you."

"Really?"

"Yeah, you deserve to have a life, Mom."

A guilty flutter winds in my gut. "I don't want you to starve," I say, standing again with the need to move my body. "You're welcome to come eat, and you know Tammy is here on weekends, and she'll take care of you."

"I don't need someone to take care of me. I'm eighteen."

"Well, you know I worry." I ruffle his hair as I spin on my heel to take that table's order. "So, we are having dinner Sunday night to catch up?" I call over my shoulder.

"Sure." He's already focused on his phone as he replies with a snarky, "Don't do anything I wouldn't do."

Speaking through a chuckle, I say, "I'm not sure that leaves out anything."

His laughter joins mine but quickly fades into the background as I focus on my table. For the first time in a long, long time, I have plans that aren't about Noah or hockey or keeping my house clean and my fridge stocked.

I'm doing something for myself.

Butterflies flit in my stomach, adding a lightness in my chest that I haven't felt in...forever.

Tammy comes in to relieve me of the dinner rush, so I'm able to sneak out early. Yes, I was watching the clock. How could I not? With my rolling suitcase in tow, I step outside. My stomach twists, unleashing the fleet of butterflies again. Bill is waiting with his headlights cutting soft beams through this winter's never-ending flurries. Tugging my pink coat tighter, I step off the curb, and a zing of nerves fires in my gut. He gets out of the SUV, greeting me by opening the passenger door. "Are you sure you don't mind sneaking around? It sure looks good on you."

"I'm getting used to it, especially since I have a partner in crime." I laugh as I tug my rolling suitcase off the curb, struggling to get it over the bumps of snow.

His grin grows as he rushes forward, taking my suitcase. "Speaking of crime, you should be warned, because I do have a small record. There were a slew of speeding tickets and a few parking violations. Let's say my impatience shows on my driving record."

"And here I thought you were a good influence." I speak over my shoulder as I slide into my seat.

"I am." He pops the hatch on the back, sliding in my suitcase before running around to his side of the SUV, and getting in. "Your suitcase is heavy. I hope that means you brought lots of board games."

"Board games, snacks, fuzzy socks." I click my seat belt and glance at him, a full lightning bolt zapping through my gut when I realize *this is it.*

I'm really going away.

And I'm leaving with Bill Baker—a billionaire—to see if we have a romantic connection.

This can't be my life!

"That's perfect packing." He shifts the vehicle into drive and pulls out. "We won't have a chance to get bored."

The drive to the airport is quiet in that comfortable way I'm still getting used to. He hums a little to whatever song is on the radio while he leaves one hand on the wheel and the other resting relaxed near the console. Every few minutes his gaze slides to me, like he's checking to make sure I haven't changed my mind.

I haven't.

He's clean-shaven today, which is so unfair, because it brings out his sharp jawline and smirk that seems to have the ability to get me to confess all my thoughts. His shirt is a deep blue to match his eyes, and it fits just right. The rich scent of his cologne drifts over, something dark and subtle with a hint of spice. I fight the ridiculous urge to lean over just to figure out what that spice is.

Clove, maybe?

No, I haven't changed my mind about going with him.

If anything, each mile we travel away from town only solidifies that I need this weekend away.

And I *want this weekend with him.*

"You dressed handsome," I say, my tone deliberately normal, though my heartbeat is anything but a normal rate.

He grins with one of his eyebrows lifted. "Well, I'm glad you approve. I was hoping to impress you."

I smirk. "Maybe it's working."

His mouth curves into something just shy of smug. "So, you have been checking me out."

"I didn't say I was checking you out," I protest very weakly, as it's hard to deny it now when I've already said he was handsome. I shake my head, biting back a flirty smile. "You're impossible."

"And yet," he says as his eyes stay on the road, "you agreed to spend the weekend with me."

"Right." Giving in with a small laugh, I fight the urge to tease him about how he forced me into this, because I want him to know it means a lot to me for him to take this time for this trip. "I'm actually excited to spend time with you."

His gaze flicks to me, lingering a fraction too long before he says in a low tone, "Careful what you say. I might take that as an invitation to like you even more."

Heat blooms in my cheeks, but I manage to roll my eyes for good measure. He takes a turn, pulling into the gates of a private tarmac. My heart skips a beat when he stops in front of a sleek jet that looks like something out of a movie.

"Wow, you seriously weren't kidding about this spoiling me thing," I say, blinking up at the plane as he opens my door.

He shrugs like it's nothing. "You said you didn't want to run into anyone you know, and this is the safest way to do that."

I stare at him, and he slants his grin into a bit of a cocky angle I've never seen before. Perhaps he's gaining confidence around me, as he's always acted rather modestly. As he grabs our bags and walks me to the steps, I can't help but keep stealing glances at him. It's like he's also peeling back a layer he's never shown me. Perhaps to get me to also trust him? I climb up the stairs and pass through the open door into what is the fanciest plane I've ever seen. With rows of leather recliners on each side of the small aisle, I follow the gold trim lights to the first seat and turn to look at him. "Seriously?"

"Don't be nervous," he says, settling in the recliner across from me. He has our bags with him. He sets mine in a closet in front but retains his bag as he carries it to his seat. "It's not any different than any other plane, but the snacks are better, and it's private but not private. Exactly how you prefer it."

"And by not, you mean there's a pilot behind that closed door?"

"And a flight attendant, but she only comes back if I buzz for her. So, it's private but not." Before I can come up with a retort, he flips his tray down in front of his seat and reaches into his bag. He removes a wad of snacks and plops them on his tray. My eyes grow wide. There's everything from candy bars, trail mix, pretzels, and gummy bears packs, and he sorts everything into two equal piles. "You're not the only one who packed snacks," he declares with a victorious smile.

"You brought enough for a long trip," I say. "I thought we were only going somewhere close by."

"Or," he says, glancing at me like he's letting me in on a secret, "this is everything we need for our competition."

"Competition?" I raise an eyebrow as he slides the final thing out of his bag and sets it on the table—a deck of cards. "Ever play Go Rummy?"

"I only vaguely remember from when I was little. I think I played it with my grandma a few times." I'm already eyeing the peanut butter chocolates. He clearly knows the way to my heart.

"This," he catches me staring at the peanut butter cups and slides them in front of me, "is the real currency." He retrieves the deck of cards, giving them a quick shuffle and then deals them out into two piles. I pick up my cards and rearrange them into matching sets, while he does the same.

He pushes forward a packet of gummy bears like he's some high roller. "Put up your wager."

It's ridiculous and strangely intimidating. I hate to give up my peanut butter cups, so I start with the bags of sour candies I don't like anyway.

His expression gives nothing away as he lays down his cards with confidence.

I follow his lead, laying down my cards. Before I know it, I've lost the round. He snatches my wager and drags it back to his pile. Then he reshuffles the deck.

"So much for beginner's luck." I toss a bag of pretzels into the center, as I clutch my peanut butter cups like they are gold plated. "You're merciless." I narrow my eyes in what I hope passes for intimidation.

He's looking entirely too smug. "Merciless?" he repeats. "I prefer the term skilled." He adds a bag of chips on top of my pretzels and waits for my counter.

"Skilled at robbing me blind," I counter, with the last snack on my pile—my peanut butter cups.

He leans back in his seat. The move makes his knee brush mine, and the brief contact sends an unhelpful zing right through me. "I'm competitive," he says. "And possibly a little hungry."

I try to focus on my cards, but my eyes betray me, flicking to the way his forearm flexes with every card he deals.

I lose again, but in my defense, it was much more of a loss than the first one because I lost my peanut butter cups. "That's it." I sigh as I throw down my cards. "I'm out. Clearly, you've won."

He tilts his head, a slow smile playing on his mouth. "You've got one thing left you could bet."

I arch a brow as I scan the plane tray for a wrapper or something I've skipped over. There's nothing on my side, as everything is piled high on his. "What do I have left?"

"How about a kiss?"

I can't tell if he's joking, but my pulse spikes from the way he's holding my gaze. "That's brave."

"Only if you want," he says lightly, but there's something in his voice that feels like a dare.

Unable to help myself, I glance at his candy stash like it might offer me guidance. My peanut butter cups are on the top of the pile, taunting me. What I wouldn't do to win those back... "Okay," I finally say, "If I win, I get everything back."

"If I win," he cuts in, "I get a kiss." He dramatically shuffles the cards. "The next hand, fate decides." He deals the deck into two piles, and we take turns laying down the cards.

Remaining quiet, we share long eye locks every time one of us takes a turn, until fate decides to have a sense of humor, and I win. With a mock-evil chuckle, I reach across the tray and scoop every last snack into my arms, and I add theatrics to my giggle, declaring, "I won it all!"

He playfully groans, dropping his head back against the seat. "You cheated."

"Did not. I won fair and square." I take a moment to restack my peanut butter cups on top, and then in a quick change of thought, I lean across the armrest anyway. His breath stills as I press a quick kiss to his cheek. I smile as the corner of his mouth curves up before I've even pulled away.

"Thank you"—my voice is softer than I meant it to be—"for planning this trip."

His eyes hold mine with so much power, I forget we're soaring through the sky at thirty thousand feet.

It's just him and me. We play several more rounds of cards, taking turns winning and losing, and our snacks go back and forth. Before I know it, the captain's voice crackles overhead, "We'll be landing in about ten minutes."

"Landing?" I blink as I cut my gaze out the window. "Already?"

Bill promptly gathers the cards, packing them into the cardboard box. "Time flies when you're getting your butt kicked."

"Oh please, I was letting you think you could win."

He laughs as he sits back, and his knee brushes against mine as the plane tilts into a slow descent.

"So." I try to ignore the fact he's not moving his knee while also ignoring the fact I don't really want him to move it. "Are you finally going to tell me where we are going?"

He just smiles, holding back all of his secrets. "You'll see."

As soon as the plane stops, we stand and head for the exit, where the stewardess opens the door. A cool rush of air sweeps in, thwarting my hopes for warmer weather. "So, we aren't in Hawaii?" I joke as I step forward.

Bill chuckles as he comes up behind me, and we inch outside. One of his hands slips onto my hip, as if he's trying to assist me down the stairs, but it sends shivers of goosebumps down my spine. "We need a lot more time than a couple of hours to get to Hawaii, but just say the words, and I will schedule it."

The steps unfold, and I stand on the top one, peering out. It's dark, with soft glowing lights on the skyline. From what I can see, rooftops are covered in snow. "I give up." I take a few steps down and toss a look at him. "Where are we?"

He's quiet, but the stewardess smiles and says, "Welcome to Québec."

The breath in the back of my throat catches. Québec is not a place I'd considered. Bill takes my hand as he joins me on the ground. "Just wait until you see it," he says. "This city is magical. Like Europe but closer."

I have no words. I just allow the runway lights to lead the way to a black car, which appears to be waiting for us. The driver is dressed in a dark suit, and he takes my rolling suitcase with a quiet nod and stands back to hold the door open for us. We slide onto the soft leather back seat, where the air is much warmer. I turn to Bill with wide eyes. "I'm still a little speechless. What made you think of Québec?"

He shrugs as he rests his arm on the back of the seat behind me. "Well, I'm trying to get you to have a crush on me. My first choice was obviously Paris, but I figured you wouldn't take that much time off. The flight alone takes a whole day."

Speechless, all I can do is shake my head and stare out the window as the driver moves forward. We wind through narrow cobblestone streets, past old stone buildings that bring other world feels. It's breathtaking to see lights draped across alleyways. We pull up to a boutique hotel nestled on the corner of a perfect cobblestone street. The car stops right near the curb, where the bellhop receives our bags. Bill takes my hand, leading me into the lobby.

I couldn't have dreamed of a more inviting place with its rich wood floors and a crackling stone fireplace on the back wall. Behind the tall mahogany desk, the clerk greets us with a smile. "Checking in?"

"Yes, please. I have two rooms for Baker." Bill slides his credit card over the desk. The clerk inserts Bill's information and returns his card back to him and then slides over two key cards. "Your suites are on the top floor. The elevator is right down the hall to the left."

"Thank you." Bill takes the keys, hands one to me, and in a voice a tad lower than normal he says, "You have your own room, as I promised. Just in case you were concerned."

We step in unison toward the elevator, with the bellhop behind us, and I smile. "I wasn't concerned." It's the truth too. Ever since that plane left Vermont, all my worries have melted away. It's crazy how leaving town does that to a person.

He paces next to me and flashes a flirty smile. "But if you need anything, I'll be right next door. Like, if you get lonely and want to snuggle..."

I laugh, feeling the release of the last lingering tension in my shoulders. "Wow, snuggling is so neighborly of you."

His chuckles join mine. "Anything to make you comfortable."

The elevator dings, and we allow the bellhop to guide us to our rooms. It's just as Bill promised—separate suites. The bellhop takes our bags inside first, leaving us alone in the hallway for a moment. Bill pauses with one hand on his door and the other hand hanging loosely by his side. "I'm sure you want to freshen up. How about I knock on your door in about thirty minutes, and we can go out for dinner?"

My lips pinch together as I'm not used to "freshening up" before dinner. That's not really the life I live. Most of the time I'm serving everyone else dinner, and I eat stolen French fries in the back room. In a way, it feels like I'm playing some sort of character in a movie, and it makes me smile when I say, "That sounds wonderful."

A beat passes, where we share a look. Something quietly charges between us, like the anticipation of the upcoming date. It sends a wave of flutters through my gut. He waits for me to slip inside my room first, and I let the door close behind me.

The room is spectacular.

Light painted walls with elegant crown molding. A king-size bed with a cream velvet headboard. Windows that stretch almost floor-to-ceiling reveal a glittering view of the city. I've never stayed in a place like this before. My chest swells with giddiness as I cross the room to steal a look out the window. Sure enough, it's miles of glowing cobblestone streets and never-ending snow flutters. As much as I'm already sick of the snow this year, I can't help but think it's beautiful from up here.

Reaching out to touch the cool glass, I rest my hand as I stare out with wonder.

This is unreal!

This feels like something that happens to other people. People who are in completely different tax brackets and shop at all the high-end places that never have big-box specials.

I've never been that girl.

But it feels good to pretend I am that girl, even if it's just for a day or two. My suitcase is set out on a bench at the foot of the bed, and I cross the room again to unzip it. Bill never gave me a clue where we were eating. I knew better than to ask because he wouldn't have told me anyway. If I had to guess, I'd say I need to look nice. I remove one of two dresses. Both are long and lean, more casual than formal, but this one is black and makes a nice dinner dress.

A few minutes later, I have on new mascara and lip gloss, and my hair is down. It's nothing fancy, but it feels a whole lot better than my diner apron. I drape my pink coat on my arm and step out into the hallway, where Bill's already leaning one shoulder against the wall like he's been waiting for a while.

"Wow." His eyes sweep over me with nothing but his usual unmistakable warmth. "You look beautiful."

I take in his dark trousers and dinner jacket as butterflies flutter in my chest. "You're not so bad yourself."

Stepping away from the wall, he offers his arm. "Are you ready for our first official public date?"

Pinching back the smile that says I'm living someone else's life, I reply with a simple, "I am."

And just like that, I am ready for dinner.

I am no longer a diner owner who works every day and doesn't have a life of her own.

I am smitten by this whole place, including Bill's sweet smile.

My heart pounds hard in my chest as I attach myself to Bill's side, and we step together on our first official date.

Twenty

Bill

Ruth grips my arm, which isn't a huge gesture. It's seriously just her hand resting by the crook of my elbow, but it sends my heart into a tailspin. She's allowing herself to be seen in public with me. Even though she knows no one in this city, it feels like growth.

I wrestled with the dinner reservations for longer than I care to admit. I want to take her to all the nicest places, but my heart warns me to start with something simple and somewhere she can relax. So, I went with a small family-owned bistro. We don't need the driver, as it's on the other side of this street. Even though it's colder than dirt outside, the soft glowing front window reminds us the finish line is only a few steps away, and we scurry across the sidewalk, not giving a second glance at the chalkboard menu outside.

"Hawaii is sounding even better." She lets out a breath as she scans the foyer. Friday-night laughter spirals around us at all the filled tables. "But this is really cute."

A tall waiter with a dark mustache and a pristine white apron walks up to us and smirks. "Ah! Les amoureux!"

My heart flutters as I witness Ruth's cheeks fire red, and she holds up a palm. "Oh, we're not—"

"Maybe not yet," he switches to English. "You've never been to Quebec before."

The waiter winks, and I chuckle just to break the tension. Ruth gives me the side-eye as her cheeks continue to flush. It's cute how flustered she gets.

The waiter leads us to a small table, perfect for two, by a window in the back. A center candle flickers as if it's on its last few minutes. The muted lighting catches copper flecks in Ruth's eyes I've never noticed before, and I can't help but stare as she removes her coat.

I swear that pink coat has ruined me.

Who knew I, Bill Baker, former NHL star and billionaire, could become obsessed with pink. It's the softest color, making me want to protect her from everything...and maybe I want to snuggle a little too.

"My name is Franco," the waiter says as he stands with perfect posture by our table. "You don't need menus tonight," he scoffs. "I know all the chef's specials. I understand completely what you need."

Ruth's eyes pop wide as her gaze cuts from Franco to me.

I smirk at her and then say, "It sounds like we are in good hands, Franco. Let's see what you have."

He nods and leaves. Ruth's eyes are still as large as saucers when I return my gaze back to her. "If you don't like it," I say, "you can order whatever you want, but it sounds like an adventure to let him decide. Plus, I know you aren't picky."

"I agree." She beams back at me. "It's totally an adventure, and I'm excited to see what he brings. It's been a long time since I've eaten out anywhere that wasn't my diner."

"See." I gesture forward. "You needed to get away from all of that and let yourself experience things."

Franco returns with a bottle of wine. The label is in French, and one I've never seen before. He pours us each a glass and sets the bottle on the table. Ruth looks at me and then the wine glass. "You first. I'm not a big wine person."

Tilting the glass up slowly, I take a sip and taste something crisp and light, and I nod. "You'll like it. It's not too dry."

She lifts her glass as Franco returns with several plates filled with appetizers: cheeses, sliced bread, figs, and even some prosciutto. Ruth's eyes pop wide again, and she whispers, "How did he know I prefer snacks?"

Chuckling, I serve her a piece of bread before I give myself one. I wait for her to take the first bite, as she's never shy about food. The garlic butter on the bread makes her eyelids drift down, and she hums her approval. "This is so good."

"I agree. The food is amazing, and the environment is perfect," I say, but I don't have an appetite. It's strange, as I hardly ate anything all day. Normally I'd be ravenous, especially for food like this, but I'm sort of numb. All I want to do is watch Ruth experience everything. It's like I'm afraid I will miss something if I look away to eat.

Franco returns with more plates filled with bow tie pasta. He sets one topped with green sauce in front of Ruth, and one with a nice red sauce in front of me. "So," he says as he waves his hand between us. "How long have you two been a couple?"

Ruth manages to laugh lightly, but she doesn't correct him. She peers at me, like she's yielding the question, and I say, "Well, officially we aren't together. It's our first real date."

"There's no way you are not a couple." Franco's brows bunch together. "Look at her, she's shining, and you can't take your eyes off of her."

I must give it to Franco as he is good at reading people, and I have no words to argue. I offer a shrug. "I'm trying my best to win her over."

Ruth smiles and shakes her head. Every time I see that smile, I feel like I've scored another point. I'm that much closer to winning her heart.

Franco spins on his heel to help a newly sat table. Ruth picks up her wine glass by the stem and holds it near her face, not taking a sip as her eyes narrow. Truth be told, I love the way she looks at me. After a moment, I pick up my glass and say, "What are you thinking about?"

"Just that I'm glad I'm here."

"I'm glad you're here too." I push my glass forward to initiate a toast. "Shall we toast to having a great first date?"

Her laughter is more relaxed than I've ever heard it. The sound flutters into my chest, and she doesn't hesitate to click her glass with mine. "To our perfect first date."

My breath hitches in my chest, as it does feel perfect. It's everything I hoped for, and it's only just beginning.

It's dark when we step back into the night. My cheeks tingle, but if I'm honest I hardly notice over the tingles that spiral up my arm when Ruth allows me to lead her back to the hotel, hand in hand. It's like a scene from a movie, the streetlamps casting soft halos guiding us forward.

Quebec is still very much awake, as window shops are lit, a hum of life spills from the bar across the street. "Should we walk around or are you ready to head in for the night?" I ask, after we are a few steps away from the bistro.

Her face lights up with excitement. "I'm not ready to go to bed. Let's explore."

Music floats toward us, and I turn my ear while I point forward. "Let's check it out."

We pick up the pace toward the rhythmic beats until we find a band playing outside a pub on the block past our hotel. It's not so much of a band, as it's one guy with an acoustic guitar and a gal with a tambourine, but their vocals sound amazing. A small crowd of people has gathered. Some are clapping, and a few of them are dancing. Ruth stops mid-step and just stares. "This is magical."

I open my mouth to reply, but she surprises me and yanks me forward into the middle of the crowd, where the music wraps around me, infecting us both with playful joy. I apparently have no ability to say no to her, because she pulls me into a dance, spinning me like we're teenagers. I'm laughing, and she's grinning so brightly her smile lights up the whole night, and the city around us fades into a whirl of color.

Her eyes catch mine, sparkling, and her lips twitch, curling into an angle that hints she knows something I don't. "You're staring at me," she whispers in a low voice as she leans forward and tilts her head back, gazing at me.

"That's all your fault." I wrap an arm around her lower back and draw her even closer to me. "You're too beautiful to look away."

She laughs, rolling her eyes playfully, but there's a magnetism there that pulls me to take another step closer. Now we're standing so close, there's hardly room for a hand to pass between us. "You think you're smooth, don't you?" she teases, all the while her gaze stays hooked on mine.

I toss up a lazy shrug. "You haven't run away yet, so maybe it's working."

Her lips twitch like she's fighting a grin for a mere moment, before she gives in, and a full smile fills her face. "Fair enough."

Taking a risk, I brush a strand of hair behind her ear and watch as she leans into my touch, even lowering her eyelids as if it's warming her. The way she savors it undoes me. I told myself I'd take everything slowly, but the cues she's giving me tell me she's ready. I lean in slowly, watching her eyes for hesitation. She doesn't flinch as I proceed to brush my lips against hers in a testing kiss.

I hold my breath, half expecting her to turn her head again. Instead, her mouth curves into the kiss like she's been waiting for it. I keep it a tad playful and pull away quickly. She's all laughter when she moves back into a dance. We wrap ourselves together, her hand resting on my chest. It's like she senses the quickening of my heartbeat. I take her hand and hold it there as our eyes search each other's. Her gaze morphs from tentative to one that's more fearless as she leans closer to me, until her head is on my chest. I tighten my arms around her and whisper so quietly, I doubt she even hears, "Man, I love this city..."

Twenty-One

Ruth

We dance until the music stops, and I reluctantly allow Bill to escort me all the way back to the hotel and down our hallway. It's hours past my usual bedtime. Except for the soft tap of our shoes on the carpet, everything is silent and no one is around. When we reach my door, he slides his hand on my back, as he's clearly gotten so used to doing tonight, and he leans down, staring deeply into my eyes like I'm the only thing that matters.

My breath catches in the back of my throat as I lean against the door. Without hesitation, I wrap my hands around his neck, inviting him to kiss me. My knees are jelly as his lips connect with mine in a tender kiss that's only sweet, and he pulls away, leaving a whisper between us, "Goodnight, Ruth."

Unable to speak, I allow him to take the cardkey from my hand. He swipes it for me, opens my door, and stands back while I go in. He pulls the door shut behind me, and I pause with my eyes closed. My heart slams against my rib cage, as the last few hours replay in my mind like a movie. I've never experienced anything like it.

Then the spiral starts. *It's too soon to be feeling these strong feelings. We hardly know each other. I need to slow down and stop letting myself be so careless. One weekend of letting my hair down is not going to be worth the heartache...*

Without turning on a light, I step forward, and my foot catches on the open bathroom door. I both stub my toe and stumble forward, accidentally hollering, "Ouch!"

A second later, my phone vibrates in my coat pocket, and I slide it out.

I sigh as I reply: **I stubbed my toe on the door, but I'm fine. Thank you for checking.**

His reply comes back right away:

Bill: Good, I was about to call the cops to report a very ungraceful thud.

I smile wide and reply:

Me: Ungraceful? I'll have you know I managed to stay on my feet, and I was rather light-footed.

Bill: Wish I could have seen it.

I grin even wider, my cheeks starting to fatigue from the amount of smiling tonight.

Me: Maybe I need to keep some things secret. You know, keep you interested.

There's a long pause before he replies: **See you in the morning.**

I press the phone to my chest, my heart racing long after the light dims.

The rich aroma of dark coffee drifts through the downstairs restaurant as I slide into the booth across from him. Feeling extra feminine when I wake up, I slip on my other dress. It's linen, but I'm smart and slip on thick tights underneath. Then I take a few extra minutes to curl and pin my hair up, leaving a few loose tendrils to frame my face. When I see myself in the mirror, I hardly recognize the face staring back, but I don't have time to ponder as Bill texted me he had a table for us.

"Good morning." His voice carries a bit of a sleepy rasp. "How'd you rest?"

"Well," I say, recalling not waking even once until my room was filled with sunlight.

His eyes twinkle as he motions to the cup in front of me. "I already ordered coffee with extra sugar. They had a breakfast sampler with all sorts of things that looked nothing like a proper meal, so I ordered that too."

Shaking my head, I can't help laughing. "Am I that predictable?"

He raises an eyebrow. "No, I just pay attention."

I tuck my hands around my cup, feeling the warmth seep in. I watch him watch me. Somewhere along the way, we've developed this hidden language that has no words, but we understand each other with just a look.

The waiter comes and places a huge platter between us. If France could sit on the table, this is exactly what it would look like. There's a small mountain of buttery croissants in the center. A perfect spread of apple slices curves along one edge, winding their way down until they brush against a scatter of plump berries.

My stomach releases a very unladylike groan when I spot the fat wedges of Brie daring me to tear off a piece of bread and try it. Beside the Brie, there are more chunks of cheese and a pile of round crackers so high, I could eat on that for a week.

The selection goes on for days, as squares of dark chocolate spill over onto a row of roasted red pepper strips glistening with olive oil. The sweet-salty aroma wafts in my direction, and I slide to the edge of my seat, as my taste buds beg for flavor. "Wow, it does feel like you understand the way to my heart. This looks amazing."

"I wanted something for us to enjoy our morning. You know, nothing to rush over."

My eyebrows tug upward as I struggle to not gush. This is a lot to take in first thing in the morning. I've never been spoiled like this ever. "This is perfect"

He laughs playfully as he reaches for a croissant. "I agree. Waking up to have breakfast with you is everything." He bites off the edge of his croissant and smiles through his chewing. My heart flutters hard against my chest as I feel a layer of my shield chipped away. I don't have much guard left around him. It's hard not to want to share myself openly with him when he's so open and generous with me.

"Is something wrong?" He quirks an eyebrow and stops mid-chew. "I've never seen you hesitate around food this long before."

"No." I shake my head and reach for the serving spoon to scoop berries. "Nothing is wrong at all."

Twenty-Two

Bill

The cobblestones crunch with more new snow that arrived early this morning, but it does nothing to slow us down as we stroll hand in hand through the winding streets of Old Québec. I've been here many times, but it's never been as exciting as this time. I love the way Ruth's eyes light up at every corner. It feels like I'm seeing the city again for the first time through her eyes. "On today's guided tour," I tease as I gesture forward, "you will see a chocolate shop and a bookstore on this side of the street, and an art gallery over here."

She laughs, nudging me with her elbow. "I vote for all the snack places."

"Like seriously?" I mock shock as I stare at her. "I saw you lick that breakfast platter clean. How are you hungry?"

"I didn't lick it!" she bites back, but her laughter takes over. I can't help but join her. Her gaze shifts to the window next to us. It's a clothing boutique with a couple of mannequins wearing short dresses. "Those are beautiful but they're certainly not right for this weather."

I grin. "You could always pick them up and keep them on hand for our trip to Hawaii."

She rolls her eyes but squeezes my palm, making my heart flutter in full throttle. "Oh look." She points way ahead to the hill where the Château Frontenac is. "What is that castle?"

"It's a hotel." I pull her forward. "Come on. Let's take a selfie of us kissing in front of it."

She grins at me, cheeks flushing from the cold and maybe something more. "That's a little bold."

"I didn't get where I am today by being shy." I retrieve my phone to prepare it as we stride uphill, until the city is mostly below us. She's practically glowing when we stop. "Let's not waste a perfectly good photo opportunity." I flash her my best flirty smile as I wrap my arm around her waist and draw her toward me. Her body seems to melt into mine, and I hold my other arm out to capture our selfie as I lean in and steal a sweet and tender kiss from her lips.

She laughs as I pull away and slide my phone in front of her to show her. "That's going to be my wallpaper for sure."

"I didn't know you were such a romantic." She gives me a side-eye as we turn to walk forward again. Our hands slide around each other like they don't know another way to be.

"I'm not really," I say, my voice coming out quieter than I mean it to. "It's more what you do to me." The words leave my mouth before I can overthink them. Her shoulder rubs against mine like it's an accident, but we both know it's not. There's magnetism between us when we are together that's too hard to fight.

My heart beats in uneven bursts, sending little flutters through my whole chest. I welcome the sight of a street vendor, and I step to the side without saying anything, pretending I'm curious. She joins me next to the displays of touristy items. It's everything from keychains to shot glasses, and my gaze fixes on a row of beaded bracelets. There's every color of the rainbow, and I thumb through them until I find the perfect pink to match her coat. With a smirk, I hold it up to her like an offering. "You need this."

"Wow, first chocolate for breakfast, then fairy-tale kisses, and now jewelry? It's not even noon yet."

"So, that's a yes, I can buy this for you?" I wink and hand the bracelet to the vendor. I slip my card out of my wallet and slide that over to him as well, then turn back to her with a flirty grin.

"How can I say no?" She sighs as she squeezes my hand, and the vendor passes the bracelet and my card back to me.

Tucking my card in my pocket, I turn to her and hold up the bracelet. "May I put it on you?"

"Of course." She holds up her arm, pushing up the sleeve of her coat, and her fingers brush mine as I join the clasp together. That small contact of her skin sends a jolt straight to my heart.

Maybe it is the city.

But something is happening.

It's clear we are both experiencing it, as we can't stop smiling or finding reasons to accidentally touch each other. We link arms, continuing our stroll through all the street vendors on the block. It's past noon before I spot a little place to eat at the corner. "Doesn't that look neat?"

"Yeah." She nods as she looks back at me. "They look like they'd have great appetizers."

I laugh as I take that as she wants to go, and I smile at her. "Lead the way."

Twenty–Three

Ruth

We duck inside a cozy-looking spot off the street. The warmth melts the tingles from my nose, as we pass the "Seat Yourself" sign and stroll to a bar-height table near the window. Bill scoots out my chair and smiles in a way that makes my tingles instantly return. He sits across from me and scans the menu on the table, and he murmurs, "Let's see what non-meals they have here..."

I laugh just as the waiter steps up. I'm shaking my head when Bill proceeds to ask, "We need something for the lady that isn't a meal. She only likes snack food."

The waiter speaks English with a French accent. "Interesting. How about a poutine? It's fries, cheese curds, and gravy."

Bill smiles back at me for a lingering moment before turning his focus on the waiter. "That sounds perfect."

He's casual with one elbow on the table, but the way the late afternoon light slides over the strong lines of his jaw should be illegal. His hair is tousled from being outside, and there's that tiny crease near his eyes that only shows up when he's happy, like he is now.

I'll admit when I first saw him, I didn't look twice. Sure, he was good looking, but of course I thought he was out of my league. Now that I've gotten to know him, my attraction to him has only grown stronger. It's funny how that works. All I can think about is how safe I feel when he wraps his arms around me.

It's absurd!

This isn't even me.

I've never been like this. We aren't even touching, but my body wants to lean in his direction.

Who is this person inside my brain?

Back home, I've got a to-do list a mile long that never leaves my brain. All the bills I must pay, the customers who need to order, and all the ways I've come up short.

Bill definitely was on to something with this trip. It didn't take long for all the noise to fade.

Here, there's just him and me.

Our dish arrives, and the waiter places it between us to share. It's steaming, the way I like it, and I take a tentative bite, but immediately my taste buds awaken and ask for more. "Amazing." I cover my mouth as I chew, but I can't wait to express my delight. "This is so good."

He's not even reaching out to try a bite. He's watching me with a grin on his face that makes my heart crack a little. Just like that, another piece of my shield crumbles to the ground. "This is exactly what I needed," I say, taking another bite of the cheese like I'm some four-year-old kid on Christmas morning left alone with a stack of toys.

He nods, eyes sparkling. "Yeah, I'm beginning to see that cheese is your love language. That and chocolate."

"I mean, it can't hurt." I chuckle as I go in for another bite.

He reaches across the table, brushing his fingers against my hand. I allow my fingers to lace between his, not all the way but into a lazy hold that satisfies my need to touch him, while I proceed to clean my entire plate, never feeling more content.

"Now what?" I ask when I've scooped off the last of the cheese.

"From the looks of what you just ate, I'd guess you are ready for a nap."

"No," I'm quick to rebutt as I don't want to waste any time sleeping. "Let's do something active."

"Are you serious?" He raises an eyebrow as his gaze goes from my empty plate and back to me. After a beat, he says, "Ice skating?"

We've already done that once, and my mind instantly goes back to the moment of our kiss. My heart skips a beat, like it's fully on board for a take two. I'm quick to accept. "Sure. That sounds like the perfect way to end our day."

Twenty-Four

Bill

Place D'Youville is buzzing with skaters. It honestly resembles something out of a Disney movie, and I feel a thrill I haven't felt in years as I lace up my skates next to Ruth.

"It's perfect," I say, tugging at my laces. "Are you going to be able to make it without having a snack first? Want me to grab you a cocoa before we start?"

She lifts her brows at me and lets out a laugh. "I seriously just ate. I should be fine. It's nice to know you think I'm a pig." She bumps her elbow against my arm with a playful shove.

I chuckle, standing as she does. "I don't think that at all. I just noticed you are happiest when you have lots of random food breaks. I don't want to have to rescue you when you faint halfway around."

"Funny," she says, but she's smiling, her cheeks already pink from the cold.

We step onto the ice at the same time, no words needed, our strides falling in sync almost immediately. My arm finds its place around her waist like it was always meant to be there, though she doesn't need the assistance.

We settle into a rhythm of leaning and brushing against each other every few seconds in ways that don't feel accidental anymore. Her hip grazes mine, and my hand steadies her as other skaters rush by. Every time I touch her side, I feel the heat of her through her coat, and it sends a charge through me.

After a few laps, I catch her gaze. "What are you thinking about?" I ask.

"Just sort of watching you skate. You hockey players make it look so easy."

"You know," I say, voice dropping lower, "my dad taught me how to skate, and yes, he also played hockey, but not professionally. He had this way of making me think falling was the fun part. As soon as I would fall, he'd smile and act like that was just part of the journey, and after that, I saw it more as an adrenaline rush than something to be feared."

Her expression softens. "He sounds wonderful."

"He was." I swallow, glancing across the rink. "I miss him every day. He worked at the lumbermill outside Mapleton his whole life. He was a humble man, but he taught me how to work hard, and he was my best friend. He passed a couple years ago of natural causes but, man, do I miss him..."

There's a beat of silence where she tilts her head closer. "I'm sorry, Bill. That must've been hard."

I try to smile. "Hard but normal, right? I'm getting older, and it's normal to start losing people. Comes with the territory, right?" I mean it as a joke, but the words land heavier than I intended.

Her eyes hold mine steady. "You're right. Life is short."

Something in her tone makes me wonder where her mind has gone, but I don't push. She glances away. I don't know what memory she's living in, but I can tell it's one that shaped her.

We let the conversation fade and just skate, her gliding backward now with me holding her waist, guiding her. She tilts her head back, eyes finding mine. At the edge of the rink, we slow to a stop, flushed and winded. I keep my hand at her back a little longer than necessary. Then I lift my hand to her cheek, brushing her skin with my thumb. She leans into the touch, and my chest tightens at the trust in the gesture.

I can't hold back another second. I lower my head and kiss her slowly—savoring the warmth of her lips in the winter chill. She presses into me, and I swear she wants to kiss just as much as I do.

When I finally pull back, we're both breathing hard, not just from skating anymore.

"This was the best day of my life," I murmur, my forehead resting against hers.

Her lips curve faintly, hovering near mine. "Was? Feels to me like we're just getting started..."

"That means you need a snack, right?" I give her a suspicious side-eye.

"No." She rolls her eyes as a chuckle leaks out.

"Are you sure about that?" I press the issue again. "I saw they have donuts with mountains of frosting on them."

"Did you see chocolate ones?" Her gaze snaps to the side of the rink where the concessions are, and I immediately laugh, taking that as a yes.

"Let's go." I push off my skate, pulling her forward, and we glide together off the ice.

Twenty-Five

Ruth

I've stopped in front of my hotel door that Bill has walked me right up to. "Never mind," I whisper into his lips that are nearly touching mine, but it sounds weak even to me. "This whole trip and everything about it was a mistake." I half laugh, but real doubts are sinking in, as my heart hasn't slowed in hours.

"Call it whatever you want, but I don't believe for a second you think it's a mistake." Bill leans closer and rasps as his gaze flicks to my lips.

Judging from the way his hand is parked on my hip like he owns it, he's feeling the magnetism I am. Instead of fighting it, I tilt my chin up, teasing him, "Maybe it's fine."

His smile tugs into one I've never seen before. It's a mixture of something mischievous and confused. "Just fine?" he whispers, and his voice comes out rough. Without waiting for a reply, he shifts his weight, removing his hand from my hip and placing it on the door behind me. It's no longer touching me, but I feel it like a spark above me.

My heart races.

My stomach loops into an endless spiral.

I'm not this person.

I'm not this woman who gets caught up in the romanticism of a beautiful city and these warm kisses and soft touches. Somehow, I've turned into a puddle of jelly.

His gaze softens. "What's wrong?"

"Nothing is wrong, but I should go inside and go to bed."

He nods, just once.

His feet stay firmly planted on the floor, and the corners of his mouth twitch like he knows there's a punchline coming.

"Then go inside," he says, his voice steady. "We can meet up in the morning."

I can see the sincerity in his eyes that he'll do whatever I ask him to. It makes the last lingering crust of my shield crumble to the ground. I never expected to meet a man like Bill.

Heaven knows, I've resisted.

At this moment nothing feels more right. "I will," I say in a concealed voice as I lean back to him and whisper, "Just one more kiss." I lift my hand, hesitating for half a second before curling my fingers into the front of his jacket and pulling him to me. His eyes drop to my lips, and his mouth tightens around mine.

I'm gone.

Maybe this was a mistake to come here, but it's too late to take it back. I'm so hopelessly falling in love with him.

Our lips melt together, and I rise on my toes as his hand slides around to the back of my neck, the other grips my waist again as he draws me to him. The way he kisses me is like he's trying to erase every second I've pretended I didn't want this.

When we finally break apart, my heart hammers in my throat. I don't move, but I manage to whisper, "Whatever happens, just don't break me."

His forehead slides in to touch mine, and he brushes a hand over the side of my cheek. "I won't." He stares deeply into my eyes as he drops another soft kiss on my forehead and backs away before I ask him to. "I'm saying goodnight now. See you in the morning, Ruth."

The breath that leaks out is heavy as he turns away. I unlock my door and slide into the dark room with so many emotions pounding in my chest, the strongest one being...I'm falling so hard, and it's way too late to stop it.

Twenty-Six

BILL

The early sunrise filters through the jet's windows, but I'm still yawning as I stretch my arms over my head and glance over at Ruth. Her eyelids waver and drift down like she's still half asleep. I reach over and place my hand on her leg. "Thank you for coming. I enjoyed our time together." I keep my voice low enough to not startle her, as she seems content to snuggle into her seat and continue her night's rest.

Her hand slides over my hand, sending flutters that ignite in my chest. "Thank you for bringing me here. It's crazy how getting away from things for a couple of nights can really change your perspective."

I laugh quietly. "That was all part of my plan."

She gives me a playful side-eye and leans closer to rest her head on my shoulder, shutting her eyes. We settle into the silence with only the hum of the engine filling the air. All our awkwardness toward each other is gone.

But underneath it all, a shift happens inside me. It's like part of my heart has been rearranged to fit her in it. It's not just a playful attraction anymore. Every time she catches my gaze, my chest tightens. Even now, as I look at her on my shoulder, my pulse kicks up from the sight of how the sun kisses the side of her face.

It's obviously too soon to say these things, but I can't go back to the way we were, where she was afraid to go on public dates with me. I don't want to hide. I want the whole world to see her beside me and know, without a doubt, she's mine.

Beneath my pounding heart is a tiny niggling. The thought of her going home and returning to the responsibilities she's been using as an excuse to keep me out of her life sends a faint ache through me. I guess that's the risk I took when I came up with this bright idea.

And it was a bright idea, if I do say so myself.

My smile blooms as I easily recall the way her lips felt when she kissed me goodnight. I'd never experienced a kiss like that before. It's funny when I look back at how this whole flirtation began, I saw her as someone beautiful and smart, and someone I wanted to spend time with, but if I'm honest, it stopped there.

That was honestly enough for me. A few playful dates or maybe even casually dating for a while, but now that her head rests on my shoulder, I can't help but hope it's the start of a long, beautiful life together

I will find out what happens soon enough.

For now, I will savor the last little bit of time that I have her all to myself. I lower my head on the top of hers, and my eyelids lower from the warmth of her pulling me in. I breathe her in, gratitude filling my heart that for at least the last couple of days, she wasn't fighting this.

She is falling.

I love watching every minute of it.

Twenty-Seven

Ruth

The diner smells exactly how it always does. A mixture of coffee and maple syrup, with a spritz of lemon-scented cleaner. Margie is in the back, already heating up the grill by the time I swap the "Open" over and unlock the door, pretending not to notice the low-hanging gray clouds looming directly above the place.

It should be just another Monday in my routine of life, but everything feels off.

Sure, I do everything with ease as I recheck the tables and restock the beverage station. My mind is here, where I'm forcing it to be, but my heart is not here.

It's like I've awakened from a dream I can still feel in my bones. I've never been one to even remember my dreams, as they usually slip away the second I open my eyes, but I want to retreat into my mind and go back to how it was on vacation.

That's enough conflict to deal with, but under that I've recently realized I've been on autopilot for years without knowing it. I guess it's the single-mother-survival mode that takes over, but I've somehow managed to go day to day for years, and I never thought about the fact that I was a woman who was created to love. Not in the way I love my son, because I poured everything into him, but in the way I felt this weekend. When Noah's dad died, I just shut all that down. It's crazy how I forgot I was even capable of that kind of joy.

And of course, my mind drifts to Bill, and I chuckle because that's the biggest absurdity of all. Of all the men, I'd have to fall for one like that. It's so unbelievable and makes everything so much more complicated since he's Noah's boss. Still, my heart ticks up a notch when I think how the corners of his eyes crease when he looks at me.

The coffeepot coughs, bringing me back to reality. I had pressed the on button, but apparently Monday is too much for it, because hot steam hisses from the back. I just bought this thing last summer, but it's always something. I frown, yank the cord from the wall, and plug it into a different outlet, praying that's exactly what it needs.

I can't imagine how I will make it through a Monday morning breakfast rush with no coffee. The mere thought of it springs a bead of sweat to my forehead, and I smack the side of the machine a couple of times. A few seconds tick by where a couple of drops leak out, and I hold my breath as it slowly thickens into a steady flow of dark coffee.

The brewing coffee should be a relief, but a knot in my chest jerks unexpectedly, and hot tears prick at the back of my eyes.

It's just stupid coffee.

Not a big deal or reason to cry.

Dabbing at the corners of my eyes, I turn my back to the kitchen line to make sure Margie doesn't see me.

It's nothing to cry over.

Things break.

Sometimes they can be fixed and sometimes they can't, but that's life as a diner owner. I smooth my apron as three regulars stroll through the front door, heading straight for their table by the window. They've been having the same eggs and bacon platter for years, and there's never a need to take their order. I jot down "3 #5 platters with white toast" on a ticket and slide it through the window to Margie before I pour their coffee and take it over to the table. "Good morning, gentlemen. How are you all this morning?"

They accept their coffee with pleasant smiles but, as always, when I serve them I feel like I've accidentally wandered into the middle of a friendly debate. As retired teachers, they dress in crisp polo shirts, and I've always felt this coffee club is basically a roaming teacher's lounge that lasts long after the last lecture was given. They rotate cafés throughout the week, but Mondays are mine. I'm never sure if I'm more grateful for their business or for the gossip they bring with them. Of course, I'm not one for gossip, but since I'm so busy, they seem to be my most reliable news source.

This morning, Mr. Crowles leans over his mug. "Did you hear the rumor?" He's speaking in a tone I can picture being his most-exciting lecture series tone. "Billionaire Bill Baker was seen leaving the airport Friday night after dark with a mystery woman, and they didn't get back until last night. Nobody knows who she is, but it appears he's got a new girlfriend."

My breath hitches in the back of my throat.

Small towns are terrible at spreading gossip, and that's why I never wanted to go in public, but it never dawned on me that someone at the airport would see us.

I freeze as Mr. Deke picks up the conversation from across the table. "Seems to me to be a little impossible. He's never had a serious girlfriend as he's a huge playboy. I'm sure it's another fling."

My throat cinches so tightly, I have trouble breathing. I back away and dart into the beverage station nook, where I frantically wipe the counter. Their laughter blends into the background noise, but the air changes behind me, and I don't even have to look.

I didn't hear the door open.

I just know he's there.

Before I can lift my head, Bill's moving straight toward me like he's always belonged here. With a confident smile on his face, he catches my gaze. All at once every bit of the dream rush I've been feeling floods back into my chest. I've got one leg behind the beverage station, when suddenly his lips are on mine. It's so unexpected that I startle and pull back, and I panic and whisper-shout, "What are you doing? I have customers."

"I was kissing you good morning." I've never seen a shrug that shows less concern as he looks at me, his gaze almost pining. "Who cares if they see?"

Caught off guard by the boldness in his voice, I struggle to find a reply, and I stare at him dumbfounded. Yes, I want us to continue to move forward in our relationship, but kissing at my restaurant in front of my guests feels like we are skipping a few steps.

The biggest one: telling my son.

Now I'm reminded of that complication, my throat cinches tight again.

"I get wanting to sneak around before when you didn't know if you should trust me," he says as his eyes search mine. "But you must admit we've made progress. I don't want to play games. It's starting to feel childish."

I swallow hard as my gaze bounces from him to the customers in the corner. I whisper, "I want Noah to find out from me, and I haven't had time to tell him yet. Just give me a little while longer."

He shakes his head, but a mischievous smirk grows on his face. "You're lucky you're cute."

The customers in the corner have refocused their attention on Bill, and I find myself switching to my professional tone, and pointing to Bill's counter stool. "Grab a seat," I say, "or no pancakes for you."

He laughs, as he's caught on to the game I'm playing, and he pulls out a stool at the counter. I hate playing this game at all, but with Noah, things are complicated. He has an extreme anxiety disorder, and he was unwell for a long time. We tried so many medications and therapies. Sure, he's mostly functional now, and it helps that he made Bill's team. It's keeping his spirit up, but I'm not going to risk putting my son back into that spiral over a weekend fling, even if I want it to be more than a weekend.

I have to be sure.

It's like he can hear me thinking about him. The door swings open, and Noah's gaze finds me first, and he smiles. "Hey, Mom."

"Hey, Noah." I take a breath, steadying myself as he strides over to the counter. Noah doesn't miss a beat, he simply holds out a knuckle for Bill, and Bill bumps his fist like they are old friends.

"Hey, Bill," Noah says as he straddles the stool and leans forward on his elbows.

"Tonight's the big first game already." Bill's smile fills his whole face. "Are you ready?"

A rush of something soft overwhelms my chest as I witness Bill launching a conversation, and Noah's entire face lights up. It's like they're in their own little world. And here I am, standing behind the counter, feeling completely lost in my heart.

On one hand it feels like it's everything I didn't even know I could dream of.

But on the other hand, it feels like everything hard is getting all tangled up together.

Things are about to get messy fast.

If I had it my way, Bill wouldn't be coming into this diner unannounced and plopping at the counter like he's part of my world. This has always been my private safe place, but as I lean against the counter, a smile forms at my lips, because he fits here.

Maybe this is how it's supposed to be?

Deep in conversation now, they more than likely forgot I was even standing here. I grab breakfast platters from the window to run to my teachers. When I turn around, Bill looks over at me, catching my eye with a playful wink as Noah turns away. My cheeks warm and my heart races, as I can't handle this kind of overlap.

I need to decide now if Bill is going to be in my life, and then I need to tell Noah.

Noah's a grown kid and all, but I don't want him to have excess stress about his job because of this relationship.

Why does everything have to be so complicated?

My head is spinning when I return to them and pull out my notepad, looking first at Noah. "Cakes and eggs or meatloaf?"

"Not meatloaf," he groans. "I ate that every day while you were gone, remember?"

"Cake and eggs." I scribble on my pad and turn to Bill. "And for you, sir. Your usual cakes and bacon?"

His lips pinch together. He has to feel awkward as I stand here pretending that I barely know him. I hold my breath, as I expect him to say something to blow my cover, but he just nods. "That will be perfect. Thank you."

Noah peers up at the black-and-white TV above them, giving me a moment to roll my eyes at Bill, and his smile seats wide across his face. I busy myself with the morning rush of customers, while Bill and Noah sit comfortably together, having breakfast. Every time I catch them out of the corner of my eye, my heart swells. I get guys can talk sports with anyone, but Bill wouldn't be here, making the effort with Noah, if he didn't care.

Of all the things he's done these last few days to win my affection, it's this...coming into my little-greasy-diner world and spending time with my son that takes my breath away the most.

I never saw Bill coming.

But now that he's here, and I'm seeing how perfectly he fits into my life, I want him more than ever.

Twenty-Eight

Bill

The brand-new Mapleton arena buzzes with so much electric energy, my heart speeds up as it takes it all in.

This is it.

The dream I chased ever since my NHL career was cut short. It's crazy how back then I thought my reason for living had died. I couldn't imagine a life without hockey at the center. Somehow the dream of owning my own team took over my mind and it was like a light, the only thing to pull me out of my misery.

Now *my team* is in front of me, huddled in *my locker room*.

The whole night feels surreal as I clear my throat, even though I don't need to gather anyone's attention. The room went dead silent the moment I walked in. "All right, guys, we made it through training camp. As hard as it is to believe, it's our first game. We want to win, but more importantly, we want to play as a team. We are just as good as any other team. You have to believe we are better. Don't let doubts take over. Let's go out there, play clean, and work together."

The guys all nod with wide eyes but are content to stay quiet. Or maybe not content as much as scared silent. Coach Carlson points to the door, a stern expression planted on his face. "Hit the ice."

Everyone files out, and I follow them as I head to my suite, above our goal. I slip through the tunnel, the thrum of my own pulse loud in my ears. The elevator doors slide shut behind me, and the hum pricks at my nerves, further magnifying all my insecurities about tonight.

Every late night.

Every sacrifice.

Every single thing I ever chased pushes into my memories all at once.

It all led up to this moment, and it's overwhelming.

The doors open into my private suite. My gaze glides over the spread of food greeting me: brownie bites, wings, cheese and crackers, chips, and a fridge stocked with a full assortment of drinks. It's enough to feed a small crowd, and my chest tightens as my mind goes to one place. *Ruth would love all these snacks.* She'd giggle as she'd sneak a brownie for each hand and then roll her eyes at me when I caught her.

I should smile at the thought, but it stings in the back of my throat when I look to the left. Then to the right.

There's a big giant suite with no one else here.

Padded upfront chairs line two rows and bar tables fill the space behind them. If I had to count, it could easily fit fifty of my closest friends and family. The arena is erupting with cheers, but inside these walls, it's stone-cold quiet.

The weight of all those missing faces presses on me.

All my life, I've chased one goal: winning.

I'm here.

But it feels a little hollow.

I pace to the front of the suite and grip the railing as I peer down to the ice below. The guys are skating and passing the puck in perfect warm-up drills. Pride swells for the fastest heartbeat as I continue to scan for Ruth.

She's sitting right where I knew she'd be, behind the players' bench, her eyes directly on the ice. My chest pines for her. It isn't right that she's way down there, and I'm up here like some tyrant king. It's the most important night of all our lives, and we're separated. My hands clench the railing tighter, but it doesn't steady the ache in my gut.

This is all wrong.

The puck drops.

My pulse spikes the way it always does from that sound, even though it's been years since I've worn a uniform. Granite Ice quickly gets the puck, and Axl, our Granite Ice center, nabs the puck and drives it down the ice.

He's wide open.

It's actually so perfect, I double blink to make sure I'm not daydreaming, and Axl snaps a wrister into the net.

It's in!

We're ahead!

My team, Granite Ice, has scored their very first goal. The arena goes wild as people jump to their feet and stomp on the bleachers. The energy is so explosive it rattles my ribs in the best way. I whoop and holler into the frenzy but even this joy is pierced by a longing...

My gaze floats over to the team bench right as Noah, who's mostly warming the bench this game, turns around and high-fives his mom. Their smiles are endless beams of light. I grab my chest as it's about to seize. Their celebration feels miles away, and I'm being kept from happiness.

My breath comes faster as a thousand late nights flash in front of me. All the boardroom meetings with inventories to make the money, the back-breaking renovations that I swore would pay off when I finally got paid. Here I am, all the lies I told myself hitting me harder than any slapshot ever could: winning means nothing if I'm unable to share it with the people I love.

I grip the railing until my knuckles whiten. Good thing the rail is steel. My jaw tightens as I inhale slowly and vow a silent but unshakable promise to myself; this is the last time I will be left out. That's my girlfriend over there and her son. I will never feel this distance again.

At intermission, I head down my elevator to the ground floor where I scour the stands for Ruth. I end up finding her still in her seat, as she seems to be too nervous to move. It takes a pile of patience to weave through the crowd of people flowing in the opposite direction, toward the concessions and bathrooms. She gives me a look filled with beautiful intensity as soon as she spots me. "Bill." She nods, giving me a formal greeting. "How are you?"

Shaking my head, I lean in close enough that her hair brushes the side of my cheek, and I catch the faint sweetness of her shampoo. My voice drops low, meant only for her ear. "I'm ready for you to come sit with me."

Her lips part as her eyes widen, and she gives a quick shake of her head. "I can't. It'll cause too much attention on us, and I don't want Noah all confused while he's trying to play."

I edge even nearer, so close I could almost rest my forehead against hers. My hand aches to find her hip, but I shove it behind my back instead, curling my fingers into a loose fist to fight off the tingles rushing down my arm. "When are you going to let your guard down?" My words come out rougher than I intend, threaded with the ache of wanting to be near her and to share this amazing experience with her.

There's a flicker in her gaze, but her expression stays firmly in place. "I let my guard down quite a bit, if you don't recall."

I laugh softly, trying to hide the sarcasm because I can't help but ache right now. "It doesn't feel that way to me. I'm up in the box by myself, and you're down here. I want to be next to you while I watch your dreams of watching your son play in the AHL come true." When she doesn't say anything, I add in a teasing voice, "Maybe I need to bump up that trip to Hawaii?"

That earns me a sparkle in her eyes as she laughs and says, "Give me two hours, and I'll have my bags packed."

"It would be wonderful, right?" We share a look that's heavy with longing.

"I want to kiss you so badly," I whisper, my throat tight. I dip my head a fraction closer, so she can feel the warmth of my breath. "Don't make me sneak behind the bleachers with you."

Giving her head another soft shake, she holds back the faintest hint of a smile as the air between us becomes charged with electricity. In a voice low enough only I can hear, she mutters, "Careful. If you don't walk away now, people are going to get the wrong idea about us."

"Not the wrong idea," I say quickly, my tone sharper than I planned, and I pause to soften my voice. "The right one."

Her eyes linger on mine, shining with that dangerous mix of longing and restraint. For a heartbeat, she looks like she might say yes to finally letting go. Her lips pinch together like she's struggling, but she exhales and whispers, "We will tell everyone, but not tonight. I don't want to steal any attention from the team. This is their night to shine."

She backs away, plopping on her seat, and pretends to check her phone. I totally understand her position, even though it's not what I want. My gaze slides toward my suite. The amazing seats right behind the goal with trays of untouched food. I can't get excited about going back up there. It's too far from her and the team.

Before I can talk myself out of it, I head toward the players' bench. They are still in the locker room, but I assert my position at the end. I'm sure some of the guys will find this intimidating. It's not my plan.

I just want to share the win.

Twenty-Nine

Ruth

The game blurs past me in a mixture of slicing skates and echoing sticks. I've sat through plenty of hockey games. Every single one of Noah's to be exact, but the tension has never been so thick. Every missed puck shot feels like it lands in my gut.

I wasn't expecting Noah to get much ice time. I'll admit, I'm ready to see him play when Coach Carlson finally calls his line. I hold my breath as he pushes off, skating as fast as he can. It would be easy for my chest to swell with pride, but this whole dream is so vulnerable. I know better than to get ahead of myself. He may have made it off the bench, but he still needs to play. He's able to get in front of the puck, but his reach for it is clipped off by his opponent. My stomach drops, but he's not one to give up. He chases after it. Seconds later, the horn blares, and Noah is back on the bench.

That was short.

Folding my hands in my lap, I squeeze them to prevent from shouting out something that would embarrass him. It's hard to watch as the other team widens the gap on the scoreboard with another goal right into the net.

Bill's presence sitting in front of me is also a gravity all its own. I've seriously never experienced anything like this, as it layers a whole new kind of tension into the air. I honestly believe he plans to respect my wishes to wait to let everyone know about us until I can find a way to tell Noah, but one part of me suspects he has a tiny bit of loose cannon in him. He may hit a point where he spirals and doesn't think clearly.

The clock ticks down mercilessly.

The goals scored are ones that make us even more behind, and people start to look bored and reach in their pockets for their keys to start their cars. Many people don't even wait until the end of the game, and they move toward the exit, as if they've already given up.

It's a hard truth to swallow.

Just because Noah made it to the AHL doesn't mean success will come easy. When the final buzzer blasts through the arena, three hours after the game started, the scoreboard confirms we lost.

All I can see is Noah getting up from his spot warming the bench. His expression is stone flat. I know him too well, and I see the disappointment shadowing his eyes. Instead of going directly into the locker room with the guys, he turns toward me. I instantly know to open my arms, and he falls into a hug that makes me take a step back. It breaks me to feel his loss, and I hold him, not caring for a second who sees it. "You played hard. That's all that matters."

"Thank you," he whispers into my shoulder, voice raw.

Confused, I lean back enough to search for his expression. "What are you thanking me for?"

"For getting me here. There's no way I'd be here without you." There's a faint glint in his eyes. Sure, it's tired, but it's there. And at that moment, the loss doesn't matter.

He's still my boy, who is chasing his dream.

And I'd carry every ounce of stress, every heartbreak, and every loss like I've always done, if it means I get to be here for him like this. "I'm so proud of you. You played with heart."

He pulls away, aiming to follow the last of the guys off the ice. His gaze wobbles from them to me. "Wish we'd won."

"It's okay. We have all season, right? We can go home, and I'll make your favorite homemade pizza."

"Actually…" He hesitates, as his gaze goes back to the ice for a split second. "Some of the guys invited me to get wings."

I nod, adding a full smile. "Go, you need to do that."

"I won't be out too late. I have an early skate tomorrow." He turns, and as he hustles off so many emotions run through me, my heart seems to putter with confusion.

I'm sad they lost.

I'm happy he's making friends on the team and they are coping their own way.

I'm so proud of him for making it here.

And if I'm honest with myself, I'm really looking forward to a warm bubble bath and some quiet time to read before bed. Do I miss being the one Noah spends all his time with?

A little.

But it's healthy for him to grow up too.

I make my way to the parking lot, being careful not to get hit as beams of headlights race out of the exit. When I finally find my little car under a sheet of fresh powder, I brush the snow off my windshield with the sleeve of my pink coat. An SUV pulls up beside me and beeps the horn.

Slowly, I turn but I already know. Bill has the driver's side window down, and he's leaning an elbow over the edge.

"Hey, you," I say. "Good game for the first one."

Shrugging with his face, he says. "Lots of room for improvement."

I dig in my purse for my key ring, finding it right as I ask, "Are you joining the team for wings too?"

He laughs, his eyes crinkling with mock shock as though I'd broken some sacred rule. "No one invites the boss." His voice is playful, but there's something there. It's almost like a nervous edge I never noticed before. He turns to fully face me and raises his brows like he expects me to know what he wants.

My pulse stutters as he waves me toward him with his finger. It's like there's an invisible string pulling me to him. I step forward, closing the gap between me and his car. "Can I kiss you now?" His voice is raspy.

My breath catches. Part of me wants to play it cool. We aren't in the building anymore but I'm still in the parking lot. Sure, most everyone has left, but still...you never know who will see, and the gossip mill in Mapleton is another level.

But it is mostly dark outside.

A part deep down inside of me wants to kiss him. I'm not trying to be a tease or put him off. I certainly don't want him to get sick of me pushing him away.

I'm all too aware of the risk I'm taking when I take a small step forward.

I lean over, expecting to press a chaste kiss to his lips and back up before someone sees me, but as soon as our lips touch, they melt together. My knees almost buckle, and I slide my hand up to hold on to the car for balance. When I finally do pull away, my chest rises and falls too quickly. "Get in the car," he whispers, but I don't have any problems making out what he says.

Still gripping the car, I take a deep breath and risk a joke, "That's what kidnappers say, you know."

"Clearly, I'm not a kidnapper." He chuckles, but his eyes never leave mine. That's the thing about him that gets me the most. As successful as he is, with all the things he must have to do, he never acts rushed around me. I always feel like I'm the priority, as he's a giver of quality time.

The tension that had been building all day from the suspense of the game, and even from not seeing him, slips away. Maybe it's a mistake, but I walk around to the other side of his SUV and slide into the passenger seat.

I don't ask questions because somewhere along the way, I've learned to trust he handles things better than I ever would. I buckle up in silence as he watches me. My curiosity prickles as I don't know what to expect from him. Instead of driving off, he looks me dead in the eyes. "Tonight was brutal."

"The guys—"

He cuts me off, speaking firmly over me, "Not the guys losing. Do you know how hard it was for me to look at you all the way across the arena and not be able to be by you? You have to tell Noah about us. I'm not doing that again. He's not a little boy. He's eighteen, and he went out with his teammates. He won't even care what you do."

I bite my lip, fighting the way my whole body leans toward him. "Not yet," I whisper, the words tasting like regret the second they leave my lips. The air between us shifts. My chest tightens with guilt. Before I can stop myself, I blurt softly, "Sorry. I know this is so insane. I'm a forty-year-old woman, but Noah is...you know, he has anxiety. I was really hoping they'd win the game tonight, so I'd have that in my pocket, but—"

"Don't be sorry. In a weird way, I get it, and I know I'm being selfish." His lips curve into that boyish grin that always makes my knees weak. "I love sneaking around with you."

His words hit me low in the stomach, bringing a little relief, but it doesn't relieve what I know I must do. I don't want to think about it now though. I have a little time before Noah comes home, and I slide as far as I can in my seat, getting as close as possible to Bill. I drop my voice playfully. "Tell you what, just give me a little more time. A week tops. In the meantime, I will meet you anywhere you want as long as it's private but not private, and public but not public."

His throat bobs with a swallow. "That's a deal."

As he starts the car, the low rumble fills the silence, but it's his hand slipping onto my leg that steals my breath. The gesture isn't possessive. It's more a reassurance that he's okay with my craziness. When he shifts the SUV into gear and pulls forward, I hold up a finger. "Remember, I really only have an hour or two."

"I know just the place." He winks at me and then steers out of the parking lot.

Thirty

Bill

We slip into Ruth's closed-for-the-night diner like we're se-cret agents on a covert mission. Truth be told, the place is always cozy, and it's starting to feel like a home away from home. Tonight, it gets huge bonus points because it's after hours and completely void of people.

She waltzes in first, saying softly, "I'm not turning on all the lights." Her voice is playful, but I can hear the underlying hesitation. "And we can't sit by a window, or someone who drives by might notice and be alarmed and call the cops. A police officer showing up here is the last thing I need."

"Got it. We break our ankles as we try to navigate where we can sit that doesn't make a shadow," I say, trying to keep the ridiculousness of us sneaking around like teenagers to a minimum.

With one hand perched on her hip, she scans the clean countertops, and sighs. "So I could make coffee, but I already cleaned it for the night, and I hate to do it again. How about sodas from the fountain, and for snacks, I have secret bags of popcorn below the counter."

"Seriously, I can't even think about food after tonight," I say, my voice playful, because suddenly I'm thinking about how close she is. "Just kisses."

Laughter slips from her lips. It is such a gorgeous sound my chest aches. She tilts her head, eyes bright. "Just kisses? Well, you're in luck. Those are hard to come by at Ruth's Diner, because you've met her, and you know, she's short of a workaholic, but recently she's been learning to let her hair down, and she has a few of those on a very secret menu that only one special customer gets to order from."

"A secret menu? That sounds amazing," I tease, leaning a little closer. "I would like that menu, please."

Sliding my hand on her hip, I brush my lips against hers. She lets out the tiniest sigh as her fingers graze my arm.

There's no mistaking it anymore. I'm falling head over heels for this woman. I was heartsick all night long while I stared at her from across the ice. Now, she's in my arms, and I feel alive again. I want to tell her so badly all the feelings I'm growing for her, but the words tangle in my throat.

From the way she kisses me, I don't doubt she has feelings for me too. It's always pure magnetism when we are together, and every nerve in me ignites.

Until the overhead fluorescent lights snap on!

Without warning, harsh lights shine on us like a police spotlight. We instantly jerk apart, blinking against the brightness.

And yes, frozen in the doorway, is Noah and three of my players, all wearing their Granite Ice jackets. Their eyes rocket wide open. My heart skips, then races as I cling to Ruth's expression. Her eyes bug out from her head as her jaw flops open.

It's clearly out in the open now.

Thirty-One

Ruth

The sudden burst of light feels like a gut punch. My skin prickles from shock, and my breath catches, leaving my lungs tight. I stumble away from Bill, and my foot catches a counter stool leg. I barely manage not to fall on my face as my heart slams against my chest like I'm having an actual heart attack.

Noah's bright blue eyes darken as all the lines of his face pull taut.

I'm first to break the silence, blabbering from my nerves. "Why are you here?"

"Uh, the wing place was packed. It was a two hour wait, so we figured we'd raid this fridge and make omelets instead." He shifts on his feet and rubs the back of his neck awkwardly. After a hard pause, he says, "Same question back at you, Mom." His gaze cuts harshly to Bill as he tacks on, "And you. And why are you two here together with the lights off?"

Panic bubbles in my gut. Before I can choke out a single word, Bill steps forward with his entire focus on Noah. "Your mom and I are on a date," he declares with enough strength to fill the room.

Noah's jaw drops. His eyes narrow as he zeros in on Bill.

Snickers ripple through his group of friends. Fire rages on my cheeks like I'm some kid caught stealing something I wasn't allowed to have, which is absurd. I'm not doing anything wrong, but even if I was, I'm a grown adult and can make my own decisions.

That's when it hits me.

All my hesitation was never about Bill.

Well, maybe some of it is, but as I look back at my life, there seems to be a connecting string, where I've always been the people pleaser. When forced with the choice between what makes me happy and what other people want from me, I have always done what pleases everyone else. Not just Noah, but for all my customers, when I'd stay late all hours of the night after working all day, because they'd come at closing time, and I didn't have the heart to turn them away. It's crazy I never noticed it before, but it's not my job to coddle everyone else's feelings so much that I miss out on living my life. I don't know where it comes from, but I draw a deep breath, filling my chest with so much air, I feel like I've been given a new strength, and one that allows me to defend myself.

"It's true, Noah," I say in a normal tone. With each word my nerves melt a little more. "I was going to tell you, but I wanted to make sure it was more than just a casual date, but Bill and I have been seeing each other for several weeks."

When Noah speaks, his voice is thick with disbelief. "I'm lost. How? When did this happen?"

I swallow hard, but Bill answers first, "It's nothing to make a big deal about or act all shocked. The truth is, I like your mom. I'm honestly glad you finally know."

Shock flickers in Noah's eyes, and he spikes a hand through his hair. "I can't handle this right now." He steps backward, before he spins on his heel and breaks through his friend group and heads out the door. A murmur rises from his friends, and they chuckle under their breaths and follow him out.

I watch them leaving, knowing for the first time I didn't do anything wrong. He's going to have to figure this out for himself, and I'm not required to change what I want to make him happy. Sure, my heart pounds in my ears, but that will settle. When Bill's hand finds mine, we don't say anything, and my chest lowers in relief.

"I'd better get home." I half smile at Bill, and we step forward, heading out the door together. Something odd happens as I glance at him. Though we've been dating for weeks, it's like a force takes over, sealing me further to him, and this is the most together I've felt. We are together in this relationship, so much so. The thing is though, a year ago, that would have scared me. It would have felt like it was dividing me and Noah, but tonight, even after Noah ran off, it doesn't feel like Bill is here to divide. As he squeezes my hand firmly in his, it feels like we are set in place to work through this and, eventually, all grow together.

Bill stops by my car, standing back like he is content to wait until I'm inside. "Will you call me after you have a chance to talk to him?"

"I can." I nod. "But don't expect it to be tonight, because I'm fully expecting him to shut me out for a day or two..."

His gaze softens as he begins to say, "I'm sorry—"

"Don't be sorry," I cut him off, as a small grin forms on my lips. "This really isn't about him at all. He will get used to it, and we will all get past this."

I open my door, and he steps forward, grabbing the handle, waiting for a moment while I slide into my driver's seat, and he closes the door for me, waving me off.

I steer out of the parking lot, feeling so much lighter than I have in a long time. Not just since I've been dating Bill. Relief seeps into my soul, and it's one that I've been missing since Noah's dad passed and all my grief seeped in, and I watched Noah being wrapped in a layer of anxiety. I didn't know it at the time, but I thought it was my job to fix him. Yes, I'm his mother, and I did everything I could, but that didn't mean I had to also stop caring for me.

My heart ticks up a beat, almost like it's whispering to me that it's proud. I've finally been given some clarity, and I'm going to be okay. Noah is going to be okay.

And if someone in my life is not okay. It's not always my job to fix it.

The crunch of the neglected snow on my driveway tells me I'm home, and I double blink as I seem to have driven in so much of a daze, I don't remember pulling on to my street. Noah's car is in front of the house, where he always parks, but my emotions stay even as I open my door and plod up the driveway.

The motion sensor on the porch turns on as I walk up the step, and I open the door to Noah's face. I'm taken back a bit to see him sitting at the kitchen table, angled in a way that he's the first thing I see as soon as I crack open the door. His arms are crossed and his eyes flicker at me like he's not quite able to make direct eye contact.

"Hey, you." Oddly, I'm calm as I set my purse inside the closet and hang up my coat. Since it's clear he's having a hard time looking at me, I don't pressure him by giving him direct eye contact.

"Question." He runs a hand through his hair, as he lets out a huff. "So, when you went away last weekend, you said you went alone. That was a lie. Wasn't it? You were with Bill, right?"

Boy, I didn't expect him to come in this hot.

Though I've done nothing wrong, my chest tightens, and I reply with a simple, "Yes."

To my complete astonishment, his gaze softens, and the tension eases as his reply comes out with a bit of a shocked chuckle, "I mean...this is messed up."

It's not funny, but in a way it's such a relief to finally be honest with him. I've never kept secrets from him, and a humored grin pulls at my lips. His blunt honesty is strangely reassuring. "That is what I thought for a long time." I nod, recalling when Bill first asked me out. "Trust me, I had a hard time believing it too, and in a way, I'm still getting used to it."

His head tilts to the other side, like he's arguing with himself. "If I'm honest with myself, I noticed something was different about you lately. You seem less stressed, and you were laughing more, but I didn't really think about it too much. I thought maybe it was because of my being in the AHL."

My jaw drops as I hadn't expected my son to be so intuitive, and I take a moment to ponder his observation, before I realize he's not telling lies. "You know something, I feel different. I'll admit Bill was pursuing me, and at first, I told him no because he's obviously your boss. I didn't want to get tangled up in your life, but it didn't take long for me to realize I enjoy his company. He seems to always make me laugh, and maybe that's why I'm laughing more..."

His cheeks puff up full of air, and he blows out a long breath, as if he's still processing. "I mean, it's your life, but it's just...cringe."

A nervous laugh blurts from my lips, but Noah bends his lips into a tiny grin. He rubs the back of his neck, and he shakes his head and mumbles, "Totally cringe."

Sighing, I let out a breath.

At least he's honest.

A mischievous grin forms on his lips as he looks up at me. "Just so you know," he says, tone firm as it's ever been, "I'm telling you this now. Whatever happens, I will never call Bill Baker 'Dad.'"

Caught off guard, a snort leaks out so fast, and he chuckles. One thing about Noah and me, we've blazed through a whole messy life together, but we've always been honest with each other, and I will always appreciate how he uses humor to help break the awkwardness.

"No, that can never happen." I'm in full agreement as I blink back at him with nothing but pure pride for that kid. "You'll never have to call him that."

Shaking his head, he pushes his chair back from the table and stands, adding, "Let's not talk about this again."

Thirty-Two

Bill

With my heart pounding in my throat, I push open the locker door, rehearsing over and over in my head what I want to say:

First game of the season, and yeah, we lost.

Morale is everything.

We can only go up from here.

I'm proud of every one of you.

I'm ready to go full motivation-speaker mode. Someone has to get these guys pumped up for the next one. We aren't going to win games and become the best in the league unless we get fanatical about this team. "Morning, guys," I greet them with a boisterous smile as they sprawl out over the four benches in the locker room. "We made it through our first game—"

Snickering...

I stop talking.

Tipping my ear toward the side, my eyes narrow on Axl.

He's talking over me to Noah, while Noah's cheeks burn brightly.

How rude?

I clear my throat, hoping to get their attention, and speak louder, "All right, fellas, let's not dwell on the last game, we need to focus—"

Axl whispers loud enough so I can hear it, "You mean like the way you were focusing on Noah's mom?"

The room erupts in laughter.

"Okay. Fine." I raise my hands like I'm under arrest, but I'm half amused at their chirps. "Let's address the gossip in the room." I spread my hands like I'm inviting them into the conversation, because I don't see any way around it at this point. "Yes, I'm dating someone. Yes, she happens to be related to one of you. And no, it's none of your business."

"Pretty sure it's all of our business when you were sucking face in front of us last night," Axl chirps.

I narrow my eyes at him, as he's quickly getting attention for not knowing when to shut his mouth. "Players who chirp their boss aren't rewarded."

The guys howl, creating a little gossip circle centered on Axl.

What is this, junior high?

Apparently, they just want to gossip.

I could yell at them to focus, but something inside tells me to play into it. A bubble of laughter forms in my gut, and I risk stooping to their level, as I say, "Look. All I'm saying is, if I play my cards right, this team might get free hot chocolate for life. So maybe a little gratitude is in order?"

I guess that's all they need, because they whoop like we just won the Cup. Axl leads the guys in a chant: "Hot! Choc-o-late! Hot! Choc-o-late!" until the entire locker room, except Noah, joins in.

I look over to Coach Carlson, who's been standing quietly in the corner this whole time, not mousing a word. He raises an eyebrow. I shake my head and point to the door. "Forget the pep talk today. You guys need to get your butts on the ice."

Laughter explodes as they scurry out.

All except one player leaves, that is.

Noah lingers on the far bench, tying his skates extra slowly, like he's planning to warm this bench all day. There's no way

I will deny what is happening with Ruth. She's the best thing to ever happen to me, and I see no point in delaying the conversation that needs to be had. I take a deep breath and wander over, stopping on the other side of the bench. "So."

"So," he echoes with his gaze fixed on his laces.

"We might need to exchange a few words."

Looking up at me, he deadpans before spitting out, "I'd really rather not."

I grin because I can totally remember being his age and would be completely grossed out if I had to experience something like this with my coach and mom. "Look, I know this is...weird. And I want to be respectful to you, but you should know, I really care for your mom. At this point, I don't see myself going anywhere."

"It's so cringey." He grimaces, like he's having a hard time hearing me. "But, whatever. If you refuse to go away, can you please try to be better at keeping that business away from me and the team?"

"I can do that."

He turns to grab his stick and mutters, "But seriously, dude, I will never, ever, under any circumstance call you Dad."

The thought is so out of the blue, I laugh. "I don't think we need to worry about that."

He murmurs something inaudible under his breath as he continues to shake his head while he walks toward the exit, leaving me alone.

Only this time, I don't feel so alone. If anything, I feel like I'm gaining a family. Not just a team of hockey players, but a real one, with a wife and a son—a reluctant son—but a son, nonetheless.

Sure, it's messy, but when isn't life messy?

Thirty-Three

BILL

Six Months Later

I'm way too early for our date, but not by accident. I was actually hoping to beat Ruth before she got home from her shift at the diner, but I can tell by her car in the driveway that didn't happen. I raise my hand to the door and debate whether to knock. There's a flicker of light coming from the living room window, and I set my gaze inside, trying to peek through the curtains. Just like I thought. Noah's watching the TV, and Ruth is nowhere to be seen. More than likely she's still washing up. Breathing a sigh of relief as I still might have time to save my plans, I tap lightly on the window, so only Noah can hear.

He looks up after only two taps, and his brows dip. I quickly hold my finger to my lips in a shushing motion as I point to the front door, and mouth, "Open the door but be quiet."

When Noah opens the door, his hair is damp and he's wearing a team hoodie. He blinks like he wasn't expecting me for another half hour. "Uh, my mom's not ready yet," he says, gripping the doorframe. "I can let her know you're here."

"No, don't say a word." I hold up my hand in a stop motion, trying to keep it easy. "I actually wanted to talk to you for a minute, if that's okay?"

His shoulders tense, and for a second I see the same guarded look I've seen in the locker room after a bad call. But to his credit, he steps aside. "Sure. Yeah. Come in."

We settle in the living room, where he stays standing with his arms folded across his chest. In his defense, having your boss show up unannounced is an odd thing to happen. I take a slow breath, because there's no easy way to do this. "Noah," I start, my voice lower than usual. "You can relax, because it's not about hockey or anything about you at all."

His eyes lock on me cautiously, and I go on, "You probably know I care a lot about your mom. I've been lucky enough to spend time with her—and with you. And I don't take either of those things lightly." I pause, pressing my palms together. "I love her. I want to marry her. But before I ask her, I wanted to talk to you."

He swallows hard, shifting his weight. "Wait. What? You... want to marry my mom?"

"I do." I nod once, because I only need one nod. I've never been more sure of anything else in my life. "And I want you to know this doesn't change your life. I'm not trying to replace anyone or take anything from you. You'll always be her son, her priority. I just want to be part of her world—and yours—if you'll let me."

He's quiet but not because he can't speak. His throat works as I see several swallows pulse in his throat. After the longest pause, where sweat pours out of my palms, he lets out a breath that sounds like a half-laugh. "This is... weird," he admits. "Like, really weird. But"—he scratches the back of his neck—"I know you make her happy. So... yeah. Whatever you think and if she wants to."

Something tight in my chest loosens. "Thank you," I say quietly. "It means a lot to get your blessing."

And of course, that's when the door opens down the hall, and we both jerk our gazes in that direction, not looking suspicious at all...

Thirty-Four

Ruth

I smooth my dress down one last time with my nerves fluttering in my chest, and I step out of my room.

"Ah!" I nearly trip back when I see Bill standing in my living room like he owns the place, chatting casually with Noah.

My pulse skitters like it's just been caught doing something it shouldn't. "I didn't even hear you knock."

Bill just smirks. "No worries. Noah let me in." He jerks his thumb toward the TV where a hockey game plays, the announcers play-by-play fills the room. "We've been busy."

I flick my gaze to Noah's, whose lips are pinched like he's trying to keep them glued shut, and his eyes dart side to side in a way that's way too suspicious.

"What's wrong?" I ask.

"Nothing," he blurts out way too fast.

Bill steps forward, his whole six-foot frame dwarfing Noah. "You ready to go?"

"I think so." My voice trails because I can't stop studying Noah. His grin stretches impossibly wide now, like he knows something I don't.

I narrow my eyes. "Okay, seriously, what's going on?"

"Nothing!" Noah practically yells, then fumbles for his phone and yanks it out. "Op. I just got a text from Axl." His thumbs start flying like the text is the most fascinating thing.

Before I can press further, Bill is at my side, his hand warm as it slides down my arm. He's holding something. A piece of fabric. My stomach flips when I realize what it is. "A blindfold?" I blink at him.

His smile turns sly, boyish, despite the silver at his temples. "Put it on."

I glance back at Noah, eyebrows raised. "Do you know about this?"

"Nope." He won't even look at me now, his focus locked on his phone like it's saving his life.

Bill chuckles low in his throat, like he's got the upper hand. He slips the blindfold over my eyes before I can second-guess. My heartbeat ticks up a notch.

"Relax," Bill says. His fingers twine with mine as he leads me toward the door.

"Relax?" I whisper back. "That's rich coming from the man kidnapping me in front of my son."

"Not kidnapping. Surprising," he corrects smoothly.

Behind me, I hear Noah chuckle.

"Mm-hm." I tilt my head toward Noah. "If I end up on the evening news, you tell them who did it."

Noah's laugh is less concealed and my chest warms, even through the nerves. Whatever's happening, the two of them are in on it.

Bill leads me to his SUV, where I get in, but I'm quiet as I try to pay attention to the turns he takes as he drives off.

"Are you going to give me any hints?" I ask as I tip my head back, trying to peek out from underneath my blindfold.

From the driver's seat, Bill chuckles, that mischievous rumble that makes my heart flutter. "Didn't you learn not to ask me that? I will never tell."

"It's Hawaii, isn't it?" I grin, even though I can't see him and make a hopeful wish. "I hope you grabbed my swimsuit from my house, because there's no way I'm not going to the beach."

His tone turns much more playful. "If this goes according to plan, we can book that trip, and yes, you need to bring that swimsuit. I'm dying to see it."

My heart leaps forward, as I seriously can't wait to go there, but I'm still so confused. After several minutes, the SUV rolls to a stop. If I'm not mistaken, I hear gravel beneath the wheels. He slips out his door. A moment later my door opens.

"Why do I feel like I'm about to end up as the missing person on a crime show?" I tease as I reach for his arm, and he guides me forward. Each step forward, I feel as if I'm placing my foot on loose rock. Now I'm certain, I'm stepping on gravel.

"You've got to trust me more than that." His voice holds an unusual rasp that pricks at my ears.

If he's not giving hints, then it's up to me to solve this mystery. I inhale deep breaths, identifying scents of damp earth and the faint sweetness of grass. I stride slowly as he leads me, and my soles continue to crunch against gravel until *a snap!*

I startle and halt on my heel, and blubber out, "We are totally lost in the woods, where you brought me to be murdered!"

Underneath his waves of laughter is an empathy that holds strong when he breathes out, "I give up. No, I'm not murdering you. Take your blindfold off."

Yanking it off with one swift tug, I blink against the burst of sunlight.

And then my breath catches.

We're at the river.

The place where we had our first non-date, and where we came to say goodbye to the old bridge.

It's the exact same place.

Only now, the bridge is gone.

It's all blue sky above us, green spring grass and water around us.

A giant void looms where the bridge once stood.

My chest tightens unexpectedly as sudden sadness mingles with nostalgia. I didn't think it would feel like this to have this place altered so much. Swallowing, I cut my gaze back to him as he slips his hand around my waist and draws me closer to his side.

"I hate that they tore it down. You already know that. But despite how beautiful it was, the bridge was crumbling and unsafe." His voice works over the rasp. "But you know, something happened over the winter, and nature took over. The grass is greener than it ever was. It's like it's preparing for a new, stronger bridge to be built. It looks like the future is bright." His gaze is on the water, but then he turns to me, and the emotion in his expression steals my breath.

"It's just like my heart," he says, voice breaking. "In the past, I held on to a lot of hurt that prevented me from enjoying life. But this last year, you helped renew everything." He reaches into his pocket, pulls out a small box, and drops to one knee. The sunlight catches the diamond with an impossible sparkle, and I gasp.

My hand flies to my mouth. "Oh—"

"Ruth, it's no secret I love you, and I don't want to ever stop. Can we make this officially forever? Will you marry me?" His voice is full of hope.

Tears spill down my cheeks as I nod furiously. "Yes!"

He slips the ring on my finger, and the moment his hands brush mine, my heart feels like it could burst. He rises, and I throw myself against him, wrapping my arms around his neck.

Our lips meet, and the kiss is deep and sweet. He holds me tight, as if he never wants to let go, and I kiss him back with everything in me.

I feel like the luckiest woman alive.

As he kisses me again with the river sparkling behind us, I know we've built our own little bridge from my heart to his. It's not steel, but it's made of love, affection, honesty, fidelity, humor—and maybe a little bit of hockey—and it's the perfect life for two.

Thirty-Five

Bill

The night air has cooled down quite a bit in the last hour, and we eagerly slide back into my SUV. Engaged for only an hour, I'm unable to stop grinning. I start the car, but my gaze immediately goes to Ruth. Neither of us has had a whole lot to say tonight. We seem to both be reflecting a lot and enjoying the time together, even if it does feel surreal. "I obviously want you to have the wedding you want to have. I will go along with whatever you decide, but if we do anything in public, you need to be prepared for the press to be there, and it's going to make headlines."

"Oh really?" She chuckles, like she doesn't have a care in the world. "I'm not worried. Maybe you're newsworthy, but I'm boring. They will figure it out quickly and move on to something that sells."

Tapping my fingers on the steering wheel, I ponder if I should press the issue. I don't want her to be nervous, but I also don't want her to be ambushed by the possibility of being approached in public, or worse, having her photo taken secretly and finding out after the fact when it's viral. "Well, I'm glad you're not stressing about it."

Her eyes twinkle. "Well, put it this way, if I have to have a few people take my photo to make a few bucks in order to marry you, it's worth it, because I'm the lucky one."

I keep my smile easy, the kind that hides just enough. "Oh, let's get one thing straight, I'm the lucky one." I focus on the road and pull out, heading back into town. Unable to resist, I catch the river in my rearview mirror. The void where the bridge had been is still a little jarring, but I'm slowly getting used to it.

I stop at the old, tilted stop sign at the end of the dirt road. I look both ways. No one is coming. Just as I'm about to press my foot on the gas pedal, my phone buzzes. I glance down, expecting a team update, but it's a number I don't recognize. I read on.

Hey Bill, it's been a long time. Some things from the past aren't done yet. We need to talk - Blake.

His name seems to pulse on my screen, taunting me.

"Who is it?" Ruth asks, her voice light as she tucks a loose strand of hair behind her ear. The gesture is so casual it might look innocent to anyone else, but I know her better. Her new engagement ring catches the light, deliberately flashing at me like a spark she knows I can't ignore.

I can't look at it without my chest pulling tight. That ring isn't just a gift, it's my promise. To her and to God, and I love her more than anything.

And Blake, texting right now when my life is better than ever, better not so much as even try to talk to her. Because he doesn't understand I would burn the whole world to protect Ruth from him. I would stand in front and take every bullet if it meant she could keep smiling that smile, keep tucking her hair behind her ear, keep breathing the same air I do.

My jaw clenches as I reread his text. There is no reason for him to bother me now. He'd better stay away from me, and especially from Ruth and Noah.

I'd die for her.

Without hesitation.

Without regret.

Thirty-Six

EPILOGUE

The Wedding

Prelude music softly flows through closed double doors, and my heart feels like it's keeping time with it. I stand in front of a tall mirror in the tiny anteroom at the back of the chapel, smoothing the lace on my new dress. Trying to uphold traditions, the dress is my something new, and it's more money than I've ever spent on anything that wasn't a car or a house, but Bill insisted I needed my dream dress. It's soft, elegant, with a neckline that makes me blush a little. But it made Bill's eyes go wide in that quiet, reverent way that told me I'd chosen right. Even if the choice was more about me than him, I'm happy that he's happy.

The air smells faintly of wood polish that only old churches seem to carry. Behind me, I hear the shuffle of shoes and the deep sigh I'd know anywhere. "Mom," Noah says, his voice low. I turn around, and for a moment, he's five again—standing there with his tie crooked and big beautiful blue eyes. But then he blinks, and there's this grown man—my son—who is standing tall in a navy suit.

"You look...beautiful." He steps forward, taking the spot next to me in the mirror.

"Careful," I say, voice wobbling, despite my best efforts to stay calm. "You'll make me cry before I even get down the aisle, and I just reapplied my mascara."

He chuckles as his hands go into his pants pockets, and he rocks back on his heels as if he's struggling not to fidget. "Are you ready for this?"

"Not yet," I say, then glance down at the bouquet trembling slightly in my hands. "I've got everything except something borrowed."

He frowns as his eyes pace my face. "What do you mean?"

"You know—something old, something new, something borrowed, something blue."

I lift the hem of my dress slightly. "The dress is new. The old is, well, my earrings. Your dad actually gave them to me the night before our wedding as they matched my ring." I swallow, the memory catching me off guard. "It feels right to wear them today. I know we promised each other forever, but it didn't happen, and I know he would have loved Bill."

Noah steps closer. His eyes soften, the way they always do when his dad comes up. "Yeah," he murmurs. "He would've given Bill the third degree."

I laugh through a tear. "At least that would've taken the pressure off you, and Bill can hold his own."

Noah smirks, but then his gaze falls on the bouquet in my hands, and something shifts. "You're missing blue too?"

"Oh, no, I've got that." I turn slightly, showing him the little sapphire pin at the base of my bouquet. It's shaped like a hockey puck, naturally. "Granite Ice forever."

Noah pushes out a surprised laugh, but I catch a glisten in the corner of his eye when he says, "Of course."

"But I still don't have anything borrowed." I look around the small room, as if it might magically appear. "Maybe it's silly, but I feel like I need it. Do you have something I can carry down the aisle? A lucky penny or something?"

"Hang on," he says, already moving toward the back door that leads to the vestibule. He disappears for all of ten seconds and comes back holding a single pink rose.

"I pulled this out of the altar arrangement. No one will notice if I return it in a few moments, and it solves your problem," he says, grinning as he tucks it gently into my hair that's pulled back into a bubble braid. "Now it's borrowed."

I blink fast, because if I don't, I'm going to ruin my make-up. "You are—" My voice cracks, and I press a hand to his cheek. I'm still taken back by the way my fingers meet the rough cheek of a grown man who needs to shave. I don't care how old he is, he will always be my little boy. My voice cracks when I say, "You are the best thing I ever did. Do you know that?"

He smiles, but it trembles at the edges. "Yeah, well. You did okay if you ask me."

I take a deep breath, steadying myself. "I can't believe we made it through this life together," I whisper. "All the moves, the games, the late nights, the losses, and now, here we are."

"Here we are," he echoes, offering his arm right as the back-ground prelude music ends. My heart literally stops as I know what's next. His eyes grow wide as he waits with his arm out for me. "Are you ready, Mom?"

My throat feels too tight to speak, and the music swells louder. I don't even risk speaking as I just take his arm, and we start toward the aisle together. The small crowd stands when the usher opens the back door.

It's a small crowd with just fifty of our friends, and the Granite Ice team. I spot Margie up front, already sniffling into a tissue. My maid of honor, my best friend, even if neither of us ever used that word before today.

And then there's Bill, already standing at the altar.

He looks...as good as he's ever looked, and when his eyes meet mine, they lock in.

Noah and I take small steps up the aisle, and when we reach Bill, Noah stops as we had rehearsed. Bill's hand twitches, like he's about to extend it toward Noah for a handshake. But before he can, Noah steps forward and wraps him in a hug.

I actually gasp because Noah's tolerated Bill well, but he's always held up his guard. My eyes tear up as I watch Bill's shoulders sag in relief. He pats Noah's back once. I hear a few sniffles ripple through the pews, and even Margie blinks a few too many times.

When they pull apart, Noah clears his throat, straightens his tie, and leans in to hug me, and I hold my breath because it's the only way I'll ever get through this moment. And it is a moment. One that will be burned into my brain forever. It's the ending of my life with just Noah, and the beginning of a whole new chapter. Noah whispers into my ear, "Love you, Mom."

I try to say it back, but my throat is so tight. I nod and mouth with no audible sound, "Love you too." He's first to pull away, and he waits while Bill takes my hand, and we step up to the altar together. Then Noah steps to Bill's side, now assuming the best man's spot, his other role in this wedding.

Noah gives me a wink like he's saying, "We've got this, Mom."

And somehow, that's all I need.

Bill squeezes my hand, and I look forward to the preacher, knowing nothing will ever be the same after this.

Thirty-Seven

Bonus Epilogue

Extended Honeymoon Bonus Scene:

Steam curls around me as I step out of the shower. I'd always heard horror stories about the long flight to Hawaii, and they're true. It's a long flight, and it feels good to shower. I take a moment to twist my hair up into a towel. I've never been one of those women who can make this look appear effortless, and as soon as the towel is wrapped, it starts to hang to one side, making me feel off balance. Our hotel bathroom smells more like a spa with the high-end soaps blending into the ocean scents wafting in through the cracked window.

I can't believe this is real.

I'm on a honeymoon with my new husband.

Our honeymoon.

And I got married again. Something I swore I'd never do, but fate had other plans, and I'm so grateful for every blessing these last couple of years have brought. I reach for the silk dress hanging from the back of the door and smile, as I'm already picturing Bill's expression when he sees it. First night in Hawaii, and we have reservations at one of the best restaurants. My stomach actually rumbles as I shimmy into the dress and pull the straps over my shoulders, making sure everything is in place. Out of habit, I reach for the counter where I left my ring, because I never like to leave it off, but—

It's gone.

I freeze. Blink. Then frantically scan the counter to see if maybe I moved it. Nope. It's definitely not here, and my heart does a swan dive straight into my stomach.

"Okay, okay, don't panic," I whisper, as I lift my makeup bag and still don't see it.

My wedding ring is gone!

I drop to my knees and run my palms over the tile floor, crawling like a lunatic to look behind the toilet...and still nothing. I push the bath mat aside, even stick my hand in the trash can, but it's completely empty.

This can't be happening!

A knock rattles the bathroom door. "Babe?" Bill's voice is muffled. "Is everything okay in there? Should I push dinner back a little?"

I stare at the door. "No!" My voice cracks. I clear my throat and try again. "I mean, I'm just trying to look extra special for tonight. You know, it can't be rushed. Everything is going according to plan."

This isn't the plan!

Time is ticking.

I stand back up, grab my powder and brush, slap on make-up with one hand while the other hand ransacks the counter again. I peek in the shower drain. I shake out my towel. Nothing, but I'm out of time. If we want to keep our table, we need to leave now. I don't want to alarm Bill. It has to be here somewhere.

"Dinner," I whisper to myself. "Go to dinner, and I'm sure as soon as you get back, it will stick out. You're just flustered right now."

That's what I tell myself anyway.

By the time I'm on the patio of the most beautiful beach-side restaurant, my smile feels like it's cracking. Sure, the sunset is golden, the waves lap the shore, tiki torches flicker, and it's all we've been dreaming about for months. I can hardly admire any of it, because I'm all too aware of the gaping hole on my left hand.

Bill sits beside me in the booth, sliding in so close, his arm brushes mine. "You look beautiful," he murmurs into my ear, and on any other occasion, the look he's giving me would send spirals through my whole body, but I'm numb as I stiffly shove my left hand into my lap and pick up my glass with my right. "Thank you."

He reaches for my hand under the table, of course he does, because he's the sweetest, most affectionate man alive. I panic, pretend to have a back spasm, where I wince and lean forward, jerking my hand behind me.

"You okay?" His brows lift with concern.

"Mm-hmm. Just stiff from the plane." I wince again for good measure as I proceed to rub my lower back.

"I could take care of that for you." He slides his hand behind me, lightly pressing in small circles, and I slide my hand back to my lap, relieved he's forgotten to hold it.

Our waiter brings out food, and although it looks lovely, it presents another set of problems. I ordered steak without thinking, and now I need to cut my steak with one hand. One thing about being on a honeymoon though, Bill doesn't seem to notice my steak cutting, because he keeps sneaking kisses to my temple, whispering things that should make me swoon, but all I can do is mentally scream *Don't look at my hand! Don't look at my hand!*

When we finally finish eating, he leans close, lips brushing my ear. "Can we take a walk on the beach?"

I've dreamed of this exact moment for months. Walking barefoot in the sand, hand in hand. This is every woman's fantasy, but the thought of strolling ringless under the moonlight makes me physically ill.

"I..." My stomach knots a hundred times, sending waves of nausea through me. "I don't feel so well. I'm sorry to be a bother, but do you think we can stop at the room first?"

His eyes soften as his brows lower in concern. "Well, of course we can. Anything you need, honey."

Back in the suite, Bill flops on the love seat and flips on hockey highlights. Only my husband would watch the playoffs on our honeymoon, but I don't mind one bit, because it's the distraction I need to slip into the bathroom.

I frantically shake out every towel again. I get down on my hands and knees with my phone flashlight. Nothing.

The only option left: take apart the sink.

I tug at the pipes with my bare hands, which is a great way to both break a manicure and prove I'm insane. But I don't have tools, and I don't think I'm going to be able to walk out of here and get a wrench from the front desk without Bill asking me about it.

"What on earth are you doing?" Bill's voice startles me from where he's standing in the doorway.

I whirl around, caught red-faced with one hand still on the pipe. Tears spill over before I can stop them and I blurt out, "I lost my wedding ring! It was right here when I went into the shower, and now it's gone. I've looked everywhere but inside this pipe, and it has to be there."

He stares at me and then shakes his head, lips twitching like he's holding back a smile. Slowly, he reaches into his pocket and pulls out *a ring.* "You didn't lose it," he says gently. "I stole it."

I blink as my eyes adjust and readjust to what he's holding. It is my ring! Bill has it. He takes a knee in front of me, presenting the ring. Still in disbelief, I squint as something is off. The band glitters with an extra row of diamonds that wasn't there before. "I asked the jeweler to add the band, but I wanted everything to be a secret. He picked it up while you were in the shower. I thought he'd return it before we left, but it took longer. That's why I offered to push back dinner. I wanted you to have the ring, but you didn't seem to notice it was gone, so I just went with it." His smile is sheepish and tender. "The jeweler dropped it off while we were having dinner with the waiter. You didn't even know when he slid it with our ticket, and I was going to give it back to you on the beach tonight. I thought it would be romantic, but you got sick, so I was waiting—"

The sob-laugh hybrid bursts out of me as I absorb what he just said. My hands fly to my waist, my chin jutting. "You *stole* my ring? Do you have any idea how close I came to dying from panic? I was about to rip this sink apart with my bare hands."

He grins, slipping the ring back onto my finger where it belongs. "Guess it's a good thing you're better at being my wife than a handyman."

I throw my arms around his neck and kiss him, salty tears mixing with laughter. He kisses me back, slow and sweet, thumb brushing my cheek.

"Next time," I mumble against his lips, "you tell me first that you are taking my ring."

"Next time," he promises, pulling me close, "you trust me a little more."

And just like that, my panic melts away. I glance at the ring glinting in the light and then back at him, smiling at me like I'm the only thing that matters, and I kiss him, knowing I do trust him more than anyone I've ever known. When I pull away, I wipe away my tears and smile back at him. "If it's not too late, I'd still like to take that walk on the beach."

Warm sand penetrates my bare feet, and we stroll in silence, letting the rhythmic crash of waves do all the talking for us. The horizon glows in streaks of pink and gold as the sun begins its slow descent, and we don't talk about it but find ourselves stalling at the water's edge. The hem of my dress flutters in the breeze. I hug my arms around myself, feeling like this whole moment is cut straight from a movie scene. It's breathtaking.

With Bill, there's always an invisible current, like gravity, pulling us into each other's arms, and his hand lifts, cupping my face tenderly. His eyes search mine, flickering with something unshakable before he lowers his face and presses his lips to mine. The kiss is soft, like he's savoring the moment.

I melt instantly, sliding my arms around his neck, tugging him closer, needing the solidness of him. My heart pounds so wildly it almost hurts, but it's the sweetest ache I've ever known. The waves crash around our ankles, spraying water drops up our calves, but I barely notice. When he finally lets me breathe, he doesn't let me go. He holds on to my hips and speaks softly, "You realize this is it, right? Not just rings and paperwork." His lips graze the corner of my mouth, making me shiver. "It's you and me forever."

The words slam into me, my heart pounding so hard I swear the whole ocean can hear it. I whisper, my voice breaking in the best way, "It's perfect."

He draws back just enough to gaze at me, and there's something unguarded in his expression, something raw. His eyes shine in the fading light, a storm and a promise all at once. His grip on me tightens like he's afraid I might slip away. "I love you more than anything in this world."

I press a hand to his chest, right over his heart. It pounds beneath my palm, steady and strong. "I love you too."

He kisses me again, deeper this time. I respond by pouring every ounce of love I have into him, into us, until my knees wobble and my heart swells, pumping right up against my rib cage.

When we finally pull apart, both of us are breathless. He grins against my lips as his arms wrap fully around me, lifting me off my feet as another wave crashes against us.

I squeal, half from the cold and half from joy. He laughs as he spins me once before setting me down in the wet sand. My dress clings to my legs, my hair whips around my face, but I don't care. Not when his eyes are locked on mine, like I'm the only thing that matters.

INTRODUCING SOME GUYS GET ALL THE PUCKS.

Readers, I know you want Blake's version of the story. It's already available on Amazon for preorder.

Take a peek at the blurb:

We had the perfect love story until real life got in the way.

Twenty years ago, I won the girl of my dreams, Lacey—but it cost me my best friend, Bill Baker. Now my marriage is crumbling, my daughter is dating Bill's stepson, and Bill Baker seems to be winning at life, all with a suspiciously charming smile.

But I'm not a quitter.

When Lacey walks out, I suspect Bill has everything to do with it.

I devise a plan to use my sports media company to tear down Bill Baker one final time.

Step one? Send my brilliant daughter to write a hit piece on Bill's AHL team.

Step two? Ignore the fact that my daughter fell in love with Bill's stepson.

Step three? Try not to panic when I realize Bill is stealing everything I've fought for my whole life.

Messy, funny, and full of heart. *Some Guys Get All the Pucks* **is a small-town sports romance about rediscovering the person you fell in love with and realizing some love stories are worth rewriting.**

Also by J.P. Sterling

<u>Timeless Christmas Tails (All Standalone)</u>

Have Yourself a Legendary Christmas

<u>A Modern Fairy Tale Series (All Standalones)</u>

Royally Rugged

<u>Bosses and Billionaires Series (All Standalones)</u>

Maid for my Billionaire Boss

Upcycling My Rig-Pig Boss

Kissed by My Billionaire Boss

Marooned with My Celebrity Boss

<u>A Heart that Dances Series</u>

Dancing on Broken Ankles

The Stars We See

A Heart that Dances

A Heart that Loves

<u>Water and Stone Duet</u>

Ruby in the Water

Lily in the Stone

About the Author

J.P. Sterling grew up watching old reruns of Lucille Ball and Mary Tyler Moore and fell in love with wholesome entertainment and slapstick comedy. She loves leaning into the over-the-top humor and full circle moments, especially if it means the underdog gets to shine.

Aside from writing, she's also a wife, homeschooling mom, a holistic dietitian, a former college professor, and lover of all-things dark chocolate.

*No swears. Just kisses. No Blasphemies. *

Let's get social!

Hey, you amazing reader! You are invited to join my private reader group for all-things clean books and friends. Enter the group here: https://www.facebook.com/groups/15008507 64081965

Other places to follow me:

Instagram: https://www.instagram.com/stories/authorjp sterling/

Facebook: https://www.facebook.com/jpsterlingauthor/

Amazon: https://www.amazon.com/stores/author/B01 N9TJXJN/about

www.ingramcontent.com/pod-product-compliance
Lightning Source LLC
Chambersburg PA
CBHW021407110726
47901CB00008B/2088